CHRISTOPHER
COOL

Department of Danger

A challenging assignment from TEEN takes Chris Cool to London on a dual mission: to search for information about his father who is being held prisoner behind the Iron Curtain, and to intercept a formula devised by an Oriental scientist which threatens the world with a monstrous plague.

Clues involving giant insects lead Chris and his Indian partner, Geronimo Johnson, to a London suburb where their enemies spring a macabre trap for the kill. By playing the dangerous game of double agent, Chris masterfully pits the TOAD spy organization against the wily Dracov combine. When these forces of evil collide, the fireworks light up the most diabolical plot ever to menace Great Britain.

Unexpected thrills and high-tension suspense fill every page of this adventure-charged spy chiller.

TEEN
Agent

CHRISTOPHER COOL

Department
of
Danger

By JACK LANCER

GROSSET & DUNLAP
PUBLISHERS   NEW YORK

Contents

Department
of
Danger

1 · Postmarked London

CHRIS COOL SAT relaxed at the wheel as his black Jaguar glided over the tree-shaded road on his way back to campus. The sun was warm, the birds were twittering, and Chris felt at peace with the world after his late breakfast with retired Professor Calvin Whinny.

"Quite a charming old character," Chris thought. In his rear-view mirror, the blond college sophomore saw a car zoom out of a dirt lane which he had just passed. It came up behind him with a roar.

"Easy, pal. The road's all yours," Chris muttered. He pulled aside slightly to let the green hardtop pass.

Bang! There was a report like a pistol shot as the hardtop whizzed by.

Chris felt the steering wheel jerk in his hands, and the Jaguar's front end slewed to the left. A blowout! He braked gently, then straightened out and steered to a limping halt on the shoulder.

Up ahead, Chris saw the other car stop. Its driver emerged as Chris climbed out.

"Don't tell me he's actually going to offer to help!" Chris thought. A nice show of courtesy, but rather surprising from a hot-rodder with such a heavy foot.

The beak-nosed man was tall and thin. Chris waved a greeting and crouched down to examine his left front tire.

"Wow!" The tire was not just flat—its white side wall was badly ripped, with frayed cord ends showing through the gashes.

But Chris had no time to puzzle over the damage. Something hard was pressing against the back of his head, and it felt disturbingly like the cold metal of a gun muzzle.

"You guessed it, bud," the man said, reading his thoughts. "It's just what it feels like, and it goes bang real easy. What's your name?"

"Chris Cool."

"Okay, college boy. Just follow orders and you won't get hurt. First, get your hands in the air and stand up."

Chris's arms rose obediently as he straightened

from his crouch. But, halfway up, his left hand suddenly stiffened and swung around at blinding speed!

The karate chop caught the gunman's arm with a paralyzing blow. With an angry grunt, the thug tottered backward off-balance, but managed to retain his grip on his weapon. He tried frantically to aim it again.

Chris's right hand had already plucked a silver penlike device from his blazer pocket. He pressed the clip and heard a gentle sigh as the man fell to the pavement.

"Should've known you weren't the helpful type," Chris murmured, looking down at him.

The "sleepy sliver"—a tiny barb of anesthetic —would keep the thug quiet and peaceful for several hours.

Chris replaced the anesthetic pen in his pocket and glanced in both directions. No other cars were in sight on the quiet rural road. He dragged the thug over to the shoulder, among some bushes, then frisked him quickly and efficiently.

A driver's license in the man's wallet showed his name as "Paul Shenko." Chris put it back, and a moment later gave a whistle as he pulled a photograph from a pocket of the man's suit coat.

It was a photo of Chris Cool himself!

The picture looked as if it might have been enlarged from a telephoto snapshot. Evidently it had been taken while Chris was walking across the campus of Kingston University, since the bell tower showed clearly in the background.

Tucking the picture away in his blazer, Chris walked down the road to examine the hardtop. On the front seat he found a new-looking scientific textbook, titled *The Behavior of Insects*. Chris leafed through it briefly, glancing at the illustrations.

"Odd reading matter," he murmured.

There was nothing of interest in the glove compartment, but as he checked over the car, the right rear wheel cover caught his attention. A small jet nozzle protruded from the hub.

Chris got a tool from the trunk and pried off the cover. Inside was a curious apparatus which included a capsule of compressed air and a plastic reservoir—still half-full of tiny, sharp, glittering particles.

"So that's how he blew my tire. A jet blast of powdered glass as he went by! Quite a cute little gimmick."

The device certainly had not been rigged by any ordinary criminal. Chris's face wore a worried frown as he returned to the Jaguar.

Was the roadside attack connected with his secret intelligence work? Both Chris Cool and his Apache Indian roommate Geronimo Johnson had been recruited into TEEN—the Top-secret Educational Espionage Network, an undercover arm of U.S. Intelligence, composed of brilliant young college students.

Now it looked as if Chris's cover might have been blown. If so, his usefulness as a TEEN agent would be ended—and perhaps Geronimo's as well.

Chris slid behind the wheel of the Jaguar, plucked the radiotelephone from its hook under the dashboard, and dialed the operational channel. The voice of TEEN Control answered:

"Q here."

"Kingston One reporting, sir." Chris tersely related what had happened.

There was a long silence, punctuated by the sound of heavy breathing. Chris could picture Q reaching for a glass of milk to soothe this latest irritation to his gnawing ulcer.

"Not good, my boy. Not good at all," Q said finally. "Leave the chap there and I'll have him picked up."

"Understood."

Chris changed tires and continued on toward Kingston. When the TEEN agent entered his dormitory room, he found Geronimo propped in a chair by the window, his nose deep in a political science text. The Indian looked up impassively.

"You just missed a phone call, *choonday*. Long distance."

"Who was it?" Chris asked.

"Don't know. I said you'd call back as soon as you got in. Ask for Operator 217."

Chris picked up the telephone and dialed. Presently the connection was made and his caller's voice came on.

"This is Nelson Hare. I'm the personnel officer at the Atomic Research Institute, where your father had his laboratory."

"Oh. Yes, sir." Chris's voice faltered slightly. Dr. Jonathan Cool had been one of America's top atomic physicists. Three years ago he had disappeared during a scientific conference in Europe. It was suspected that he had been kidnapped by enemy agents.

Father and son had been extremely close ever since the death of Chris's mother during his boyhood. The youth had vowed to find him, and this was one of Chris's main reasons for becoming a TEEN agent.

"Something rather odd has come up," Hare went on. "We've received a letter for you, Chris, addressed in care of your father here at the Institute."

"What!" Chris was startled. Surely no friend or relative was still unaware of Dr. Cool's disappearance. Or could it be that the letter came from someone *involved* in the mystery? "Does the envelope show any return address, sir?"

"None. But it's postmarked London." Hare hesitated before saying tactfully, "If the letter should—er—contain any clue to your father's fate, we trust you'll inform the FBI."

"Definitely!"

"Good. Shall I forward the letter to you by special delivery?"

"No. Hold it, please. I'll drive there this afternoon and pick it up in person."

Chris hung up and told Geronimo the news. "Want to come along, redskin?" he asked.

"Sure. Nothing important scheduled this afternoon."

In five minutes the boys were on their way. As the Jaguar sped north along the Garden State Parkway, Chris related the roadside attack by the thug.

"That makes two surprises you've had today, *choonday.*"

"So it does," Chris said thoughtfully. Was their occurrence, one after the other, a mere coincidence—or were they connected somehow?

As the boys talked, their conversation soon switched to the Apache language. Chris, a gifted linguist, spoke the Indian tongue fluently, and more than once it had proved a useful oral code, uncrackable by enemy eavesdroppers.

They turned east to cross the George Washington Bridge, and rolled on through New York and Connecticut into Massachusetts. The Atomic Research Institute was located on the outskirts of Boston, among the numerous "think factories" along Route 128.

It was past four-thirty when they arrived at the sprawling white concrete building with its domed reactor. Chris gave his name to the reception clerk, and presently the boys were taken to the Personnel Department. Chris noticed two security guards standing at the door.

Nelson Hare's secretary, an attractive brunette, gave the boys an odd glance before ushering them into her boss's office. Hare rose from his desk as they entered. He was a stocky man with horn-rimmed glasses, new to the Institute since Dr. Cool's disappearance.

Chris said, "I'm Chris Cool, sir. I've come for that letter addressed in care of my father. This is my roommate Geronimo Johnson."

"Indeed?" Hare's face was stony as he pressed a button on his desk.

The two security guards came hurrying into the glass-partitioned office. Each gripped one of the boys by the arm.

"You're both being placed under arrest," Hare said, "and I suggest that you create no disturbance!"

2 · The Shack on the Cliff

CHRIS AND GERONIMO could easily have sent the guards flying, but the TEEN agents were more surprised than angry.

Chris said, "Maybe you'd better tell us what this is all about, Mr. Hare."

"I intend to. Then you had better do some fast talking to explain this masquerade!"

"Masquerade?"

"That's what I said. Your timing's a bit late. The real Chris Cool arrived here an hour ago to pick up that letter."

Chris shot a startled glance at Geronimo.

The Apache shrugged, his obsidian black eyes showing no expression. "That's how the medicine ball bounces, *choonday*. Looks as if somebody has pulled a fast one."

Chris turned back to Nelson Hare. "There's been a masquerade, all right, and you fell for it. What sort of identification did he have?"

"The best. Not only a driver's license, but a United States passport." Hare frowned. "I must admit, you do bear a fairly close resemblance."

"If you mean a resemblance to Chris Cool, I should since I *am* Chris Cool!"

The TEEN agent produced his own driver's license and his university ID card. "Call the Dean of Students at Kingston, if you like," Chris added, "and I'll talk to him. Better yet—is Dr. Mitsubi still on the staff here?"

"Well—er—yes." Hare now seemed less sure of himself. "Would he be able to identify you?"

"I'm quite sure he would, although it's been three years since we met. But I often saw him when he was working with my father on those neutrino experiments."

Dr. Mitsubi was sent for and soon arrived. He was a small, elderly Japanese-American.

"*Doshiteru, pain-appuru?*" Chris greeted him.

Mitsubi burst into a beaming, toothy smile. "Chris! My dear boy! How are you?"

The two embraced and burst into a flood of Japanese, mixed with American slang.

Nelson Hare interrupted with a cough. "Excuse me for asking, Dr. Mitsubi, but is this young man really the son of Dr. Jonathan Cool?"

Mitsubi stared at him. "Are you serious? Of

course he's the son of Dr. Cool! Who do you think we've been talking about just now?"

Hare reddened and explained, "You see, it's very important to be sure of his identity."

"Well, you can take it from me, this lad's the McCoy," said Dr. Mitsubi. "I taught him most of his Japanese. And I'm quite sure nobody else would know that we used to greet each other by saying, 'How goes it, Old Pineapple?' "

"Well—!" Hare turned redder than ever and cleared his throat. "I can see that there certainly has been a mistake, and I do apologize."

"Never mind all that," said Chris. "Who else knew of that letter and your phone call to me?"

"Nobody knew of both, except myself and the Institute Director. And, of course, my secretary, Miss Arkin. But I hope you're not suggesting that *she* . . ." Hare's voice trailed off and he frowned worriedly.

It was now five o'clock. Through the glass partition, Chris could see the brunette clearing her desk and preparing to leave.

"How long has she worked here?" he asked.

"About six months. And she received security clearance." Hare rubbed his jaw thoughtfully. "Now that I come to think of it, she's been acting rather oddly the past few weeks."

"Call her in, please," Chris said.

Miss Arkin was hastily touching up her face.

Hare stabbed the intercom button. "Would you step in a moment please, Miss Arkin?"

The secretary came into the office, clutching her open handbag. Her expression was slightly wary.

"Did you inform anyone about that letter for Christopher Cool, or my phone conversation with him?" Hare asked bluntly.

"Why—why, no—I—" As she spoke, Miss Arkin was fumbling in her purse. Suddenly she pulled out her lipstick, yanked off the cap, and hurled the case to the floor.

Geronimo dived to intercept it, but too late.

Boom! A sharp explosion shattered the glass partitions and a dense cloud of pink smoke billowed in all directions!

In the confusion, Miss Arkin dashed through the doorway to the outer office. Chris barely managed to grab her arm. *Wham!* Her handbag hit him hard in the face, but he hung on and yelled, "Outside! Everyone!"

Coughing and clutching handkerchiefs to their faces, the whole group poured out to the corridor, where Chris turned his kicking, clawing prisoner over to the security guards.

Twenty minutes passed before calm had been restored and exhaust fans had cleared the office of smoke. Miss Arkin, stony-faced and handcuffed, was taken to the Security Department.

Meanwhile, Chris and Geronimo—without

bothering with formalities—were ransacking her desk for clues. The only promising lead seemed to be a telephone number jotted on her desk calendar. Neither Hare nor the plant switchboard operator could identify it.

Chris picked up a telephone and dialed TEEN's outside line in New York. "This is Chris Cool," he said tersely. "Student at Kingston—I play on the Q varsity team. I have a phone number I'd like traced. Fast, please."

Hare eyed him curiously as he hung up. "Who was that you called?"

"A friend at one of the federal agencies."

In minutes TEEN reported back. "That's a pay phone at Tad's diner on Cliff Shore Road in Whittley, Maine. Whittley's a small village on the coast. Do you want exact directions?"

"Don't bother. I can find it on a road map."

By six-thirty the Jaguar was speeding north from Boston.

"How do you read the smoke, *choonday?*" Geronimo asked.

"Hare says the letter arrived in this morning's mail," Chris began thoughtfully.

"And the Arkin squaw tipped somebody off that it was here."

Chris nodded. "Her control probably told her to report back on what Hare did with it."

"In the meantime," Geronimo speculated, "your helpful buddy, Paul Shenko, was supposed to take care of you so you'd have no chance to claim the letter and foul up their plans."

"Right. Then after Hare talked to me on the phone, the secretary called that Maine number again and told them I was coming this afternoon to pick it up."

"So the phony Chris Cool charged in to grab it before you got there."

"Exactly. Which means," Chris reasoned, "that she may have called this number between twelve and three-thirty."

It was nearly eight o'clock when they pulled up outside Tad's diner, a weather-beaten clapboard building with an antique gasoline pump. The place was empty of customers as the boys went in and took stools at the counter.

A skinny man in a stained apron, presumably Tad himself, eyed them without much interest.

"Get a lot of business here?" Chris inquired.

"Some."

"I see you have a pay phone."

"Ayuh."

"Do people ever come in here to *receive* calls on that phone?"

"Sometimes."

"How about this afternoon? Was anyone hanging around, waiting for a call?"

Tad helped himself to a toothpick. "What're you fellers?"

"Interested."

"Figger on orderin' anything?"

"Two coffees." Chris put a five-dollar bill on the counter. "And keep the change."

Tad slowly drew the coffee from a battered urn. "Now that I recollect, there *was* a feller took a call in here this afternoon."

"Do you know who he was?"

"Not by name, but I've seen him before. Him an' another feller moved into an old shack down the coast a couple weeks ago."

"How would we get there?" Chris asked.

"Take the dirt road turnoff near the village signpost. Lead you right past the place."

"Thanks." The boys gulped their coffee and left.

The dirt road meandered along the brow of a hill overlooking the ocean. About two miles from the village they glimpsed the lighted shack, perched on a wooded point jutting into the sea. Chris parked off the road, and the two TEEN agents started toward the cabin.

It was old and dilapidated. The front was screened by bushes, and one side was bordered by a dense tangle of trees and underbrush. But the other side of the shack, edging the cliff, offered a clear approach to an open window.

The boys moved cautiously, careful to avoid the scrape of gravel or crackle of brush.

"Watch your step, *choonday*," Geronimo whispered.

Only a narrow shelf of level ground separated the wall of the cabin from the steep, rocky slope running down to the water's edge.

Creeping on all fours, they picked their way along the brink, then rose to a half-crouch and peered through the window.

Inside were two men. One, swarthy and bald-headed, was seated at a portable radio transceiver with a whip antenna, jotting down a transmission. Presently he keyed a response, pulled off his headphones, and handed the message to his burly, sandy-haired partner.

"What's it mean, Mac?" the operator asked.

"Gimme a chance to decode first."

The sandy-haired man frowned over the message as he wrote down the translation. Then he read it aloud: "'Cool taking off nine-thirty tonight. Report at once if shipment arrives.'"

Chris tensed as he heard his own name spoken. An instant later came a faint rustling noise overhead.

It was a bat fluttering down from its roost under the eaves! Chris flung up a hand to fend it off as the creature's wings brushed his face. But the movement threw him off-balance.

"Yiyeee!" His stifled gasp turned to a yell as he toppled down the slope!

3 · Red Flashes

CHRIS LANDED HARD on the stony hillside and rolled down in a noisy avalanche of gravel. Clawing wildly for a handhold, he managed to grab a clump of brush and brought himself to a wrenching halt.

The fall had left him stunned, and every muscle in his body ached. He lay still for a moment, panting and trying to collect his wits.

The sound of a shot snapped him back to alertness. The two men had come rushing out at the sound of his yell. Geronimo whirled to deal with them. As Mac, the sandy-haired man, rounded the corner of the shack, the Apache felled him with a karate chop.

Mac toppled backward against his swarthy

companion, who fired blindly and missed. Chris saw the three figures above in the light from the cabin windows. Before the swarthy man could recover and take better aim, Chris whipped out his anesthetic pen.

Zip! A sleepy sliver crumpled the gunman. He would be unconscious for hours.

Chris clambered upward. Geronimo gave him a hand as he reached the ledge bordering the shack.

"Nice going, white eyes," said the Indian. "I think you saved me a puncture."

"But next time watch my step, eh?"

"It might help. Lend a hand here."

The boys lugged the men into the shack. The sandy-haired one was coming to. Geronimo took out what looked like a small first-aid bandage in a cellophane wrapper and taped his wrists behind him. The bandage was actually an emergency handcuff, carried by all TEEN agents.

"Who're you guys?" Mac snarled sullenly. "You can't get away with this!"

Chris grinned. "Call it a citizen's arrest."

"For what?"

"To start with, you can explain to the FCC why you're using a short-wave rig to receive code messages. Hm! Let's see. Add to that, material witness in a conspiracy to commit fraud —maybe even robbing the United States Mails."

The sandy-haired man glared in helpless fury,

while Chris and Geronimo looked around the cabin. It was furnished with an old table and chairs, a cast-iron stove, an ice chest, a shelf of supplies and three camp cots.

"*Three* cots," Geronimo muttered in Apache.

"That figures," Chris said. "The third one is probably for the phony who copped the letter."

On a window sill in the rear wall of the cabin was a small boxlike electrical device. From this protruded a metal tube which curved to point directly seaward through the open window. Chris unscrewed the cover. Inside was a transistor assembly with a small slab of crystal.

"An ultrasonic oscillator," he murmured thoughtfully.

"What do you suppose it's for, *choonday?*"

"That's an interesting question, which I am not prepared at the moment to answer. For that matter, what are *these* gadgets? Portable chicken coops?" Chris pointed to three wire-mesh, cage-like contraptions, about the size of orange crates, which were lying on the floor.

Geronimo picked one up and examined it. At one end was a sort of sliding gate, which could be raised or lowered. He frowned and shrugged.

Chris shot a glance at the two prisoners. "Well, anyhow, keep an eye on these characters, Gerry. I'd better go call the boss-man."

He brushed off his rumpled clothes and left the shack. Over the Jaguar's radiotelephone he contacted TEEN Control. Q listened grumpily to his report.

"If I might suggest, sir—" Chris added.

"Go on."

"With regard to the first sentence of that code message, *Cool taking off nine-thirty tonight.* It could mean the impostor's boarding a plane, possibly for London, since that's where the letter came from. So it might be a good idea to have all airports watched."

Q snorted sarcastically. "Keen thinking, Kingston One. The notion would never have occurred to me."

Chris thought it wise to make no reply.

"Are you still there, Mr. Bond?"

"Yes, sir."

"Well, stay there with your two prisoners. I'll send an aircraft to pick them up."

"Understood."

Grinning, Chris made his way back toward the shack. Suddenly he froze to a standstill. A glimmer of red light had just flashed across the water, evidently from a ship standing somewhere offshore. Three more flashes followed, then darkness. After a pause, the four red flashes were repeated.

Chris broke into a run, calling, "Hey, Gerry!"

The Indian appeared quickly in the doorway of the shack. "What's wrong?"

"Dig those blinker signals!"

The red light was flashing again. Geronimo scowled in puzzlement for a moment, then dashed into the cabin. Chris tagged after him.

"What are you going to do, Gerry?"

The Apache was switching on the transceiver. "Monitor the short-wave bands. They may be trying to raise the shack on radio."

"Good idea." On a sudden hunch, Chris strode to the seaward window and flipped a toggle switch on the ultrasonic oscillator. "Maybe the ship's waiting for *this* kind of response," he conjectured.

Through its tubular horn, the oscillator would beam out waves of ultrasound, too high-pitched for human hearing.

But the red flashes had ceased. Several minutes went by with no further signals. Finally Geronimo wrenched off the headset in disgust. "We're wasting our time."

"That's no loss," Chris said. "We may be stuck out here for an hour or so. Q's sending a copter to pick up the—"

He broke off at an ominous buzzing noise. Chris gaped out the window. Something was zooming in on the cabin, through the darkness— more than one! But what were they? Birds?

An instant later came the answer—*whoosh!* An enormous hornet, as big as a hawk, sailed in through the open window! Two more followed!

Both boys fell back as the huge creatures

swooped and circled about the room. The hornets seemed to concentrate their dive-bombing runs on a point near the window.

"*Ai!*" Geronimo's eyes were wide with disbelief. "We're seeing them, so they must be real. Where did they come from?"

"The ship! They must have homed in on the ultrasonic beam!" Chris guessed.

Suddenly he snapped his fingers. "That's what the cages are for!"

"You mean, to snare the hornets?"

"Sure. These two jokers were expecting them. The hornets must be the 'shipment' that the code message referred to!"

The sandy-haired prisoner's furious scowl seemed to confirm Chris's guess.

Geronimo eyed the monstrous insects warily, then plucked out his anesthetic pen. *Zing!* He nailed one of the swooping hornets with a sleepy sliver, and it plopped to the floor.

"Brilliant idea, redskin." Chris followed suit and brought down another monster, while his buddy dropped the third. "Never thought we'd be using these as ack-ack weapons."

The boys lifted the hornets into the cages and fastened the sliding gates securely.

It was past nine-thirty when a sleek VTOL craft, winged and with a rotor, finally hovered down on the roadway near the cabin. Chris had guided it in by flashlight signals. He grinned in surprise as a Negro stepped out of the cockpit, clad in a flight suit.

"Beau!"

"Hiya, cool one! How about the next dance?" Grabbing Chris by the waist, the Negro waltzed him about the clearing.

Beauregard Tatum, late of Mississippi and currently of Harvard, was one of TEEN's most remarkable agents. Six-feet-four in height, and two hundred and seventy pounds of solid muscle, he did his best to disguise a brilliant mind with an air of flamboyant foolery.

"New gyrodyne, I see," Chris said, gesturing toward the aircraft.

"Yeah, man. Latest addition to Q's air fleet. I just got checked out in it, so they told me to come get you two. What cooks?"

"You wouldn't believe me if I told you."

They walked toward the shack. Following Chris inside, Beau glanced at the prisoners, then said to Geronimo, " 'Lo there, colored boy!"

The copper-skinned Apache emitted one of his rare chuckles. "Watch that kind of talk!"

Beau gaped in surprise at the caged hornets. "Man, oh man! What have you cats been breeding up here—live missiles? I knew the mosquitoes came big in the Maine woods, but nothing like this!"

"Almost big enough to tackle you, baby," said Chris. "But don't ask us how come. All we did was shoot them down."

Beau nodded thoughtfully after hearing what had happened. "Interesting. Very interesting, indeed. Well, you two take the cages and the ultrasonic gear. I'll handle our guests."

After hoisting the unconscious man over his shoulder, Beau collared the sandy-haired prisoner with one huge paw and jerked him to his feet. "Come along, buster. We're going bye-bye."

Beau added to Chris and Geronimo, "Oh, by the way, in case I forgot to mention, you two are coming along with me. Dunno what's up, but the joint seems to be jumpin'. The Great White Father wants you back at headquarters pronto! Your car will be picked up later."

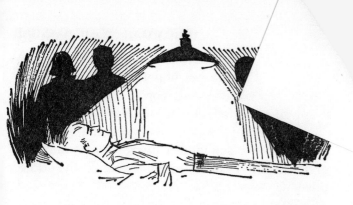

4 · A Dead Man Talks

LIKE A HUGE insect, the gyrodyne fluttered down through the darkness to a flat-roofed building in midtown Manhattan. As it settled to rest, the green landing lights blinked off abruptly.

At street level was a showroom full of foreign sports cars, with a sign: LUXURY MOTORS, INC. This was cover for the headquarters of TEEN.

Chris glanced at his wrist watch as they all climbed out. It was almost eleven-fifteen. Two guards took charge of the prisoners. Then Beau resumed his seat at the controls and waved as the gyrodyne started to rise.

"So long, you Kingston cats!"

"Ciao, baby!"

The group descended from the roof in an elevator. Chris and Geronimo got off at the top floor. Most of the personnel were gone for the night and the carpeted corridor was silent except for a muted clatter of teletype machines.

The two boys walked to a paneled door. An electronic eye sounded a buzzer inside and the green light flashed promptly and the door opened.

"Come in, come in!"

It was all much as usual—Q hunched at his desk in a navy-blue blazer and open-necked shirt, a beat-up yachting cap on his head, and a pipe sticking out of his gray-blond whiskers. His manner seemed brisk and cheery, and the bottle of milk for his ulcer was missing from its spot beside the TV monitor.

"Quite an interesting little problem we have here, eh?" Q sprang up from his desk, rubbing his palms together like a Boy Scout twirling a fire stick. "I find it most intriguing."

"You mean the problem of the faker who impersonated me at the Institute?" Chris asked.

"Precisely. I mean to say, what's behind it all, eh? Our job—to find out." Q paused to stir up the embers in his pipe. "First of all, we picked that faker up at Kennedy Airport. He was about to board a BOAC flight for London. He was carrying a false passport and various other items of identification—all made out in the name Chris Cool."

"And he looked like me?" Chris queried.

"Very much so, as you'll see shortly."

"Was he carrying the letter he got at the Institute?" Geronimo asked.

"Luckily, yes." Q handed it over. The letter read:

Dear Christopher Cool:

I may be able to supply information of great importance to you.

If you are interested, I suggest you come to London at once. A room will be reserved for you at the Thackeray Arms Hotel.

You will be contacted there.

Dracov

Chris's pulse throbbed with excitement. "Information of great importance" must surely refer to his father—especially since the letter had been sent care of Dr. Jonathan Cool! Or was he building too much hope on a mere guess?

"Any idea who this Dracov may be, sir?" Geronimo asked.

Q nodded, puffing his pipe. "Yes. We have quite a file on Dracov. Master spy. Unknown nationality. No physical description, unfortunately. At present he runs the Dracov Network."

"The Dracov Network?" Chris frowned, recalling the name vaguely from TEEN reports.

"It's a free-lance espionage outfit," Q explained, "working both sides of the street. I dare say Cloak and Dagger has employed it once or twice"—this was Q's pet name for the Central Intelligence Agency—"and so has the opposition. More often than we have, I suspect."

"What about this fake Chris Cool, sir?" Geronimo asked. "Have you identified *him* yet?"

"No difficulty there. Took his fingerprints and the FBI computered them at once. He's a vicious hood named Vinny Gorse, age twenty-five. Wanted on eight counts in California and Nevada. In fact, there's a fifty-thousand-dollar reward for his arrest."

Q coughed delicately and added, "You'll get none of it, of course."

"Of course." Chris went on, "And this character just happened to look like me?"

"Not quite. Oh, there was some resemblance— lean, youthful, same height and build. But in Gorse's FBI mug shots, he's brunet and his face looks somewhat different. He's evidently had a bit of plastic surgery and a hair-dye job.

"Another interesting point." Q frowned and rubbed the bowl of his pipe against his whiskery cheek. "When we pulled him in, he was calm, quiet-spoken—almost indifferent to being arrested. But his police record lists him as violent and emotional."

A buzzer sounded on the desk. Q pressed an intercom button. "Q here."

"The prisoner is now ready for interrogation," said a voice from the intercom.

"Good! We'll be right down."

The boys accompanied their chief down one floor to a green-padded double door which bore a sign: PSYCHOLOGICAL LABORATORY.

Inside, a white-coated man nodded to Q. "He's been given electronic brain-wave tranquilizing and an injection of sodium pentothal. You'll find him quite ready to talk."

Vinny Gorse lay peacefully on a cot, eyes closed, under a frosted white light. A pair of electrodes were strapped to his temples, and his right shirtsleeve had been rolled up.

Chris had been prepared for a resemblance, but the effect was still unnerving. It was almost like seeing himself on the interrogation couch.

"Now then, my boy," Q addressed the prisoner in a fatherly tone, "are we quite comfortable?"

"Oh, yes."

"Tell me who you are."

"I'm TOAD courier AJ-9. My control is Nikos, the East Coast boss of North American TOAD."

Chris shot a startled glance at Geronimo. TOAD was the most feared criminal organization in the world, with tentacles reaching into every continent and country!

"And who are you *really?*" Q went on. "I mean, your name and so on."

"Christopher Cool. I'm a student at Kingston University and the son of Dr. Jonathan Cool."

"You're quite sure of that?"

"Of course I'm sure. I ought to know my own name, don't you think?"

"Just wanted to see if you were positive of your identity, that's all."

"Don't worry, I'm positive. I can tell you all about my background, my classes, my family."

"Quite so. I'll take your word for it," Q said soothingly. "Now then, why were you taking that plane for London?"

"Well . . . I'm not sure I ought to tell you."

"It's all right," Q assured him. "I'm a close friend of Nikos, very close."

"Well, okay then. He's sending me to London to see a man named Eli Lustig tomorrow night."

"Eli Lustig?"

"Yes. He lives at 98 Hatton Garden, London, E.C. 1. I'm to pick up a package from him."

"What's in the package?"

"Nikos didn't say."

"And how'll you recognize each other?"

"Easy. I'm to tell him I'm interested in insects. Then he'll say, 'What kind?' And I'm supposed to reply, '*Rare* insects.'"

"I see." Q nodded approvingly. "And after you receive the package, what then?"

"Bring it back here to Nikos."

"Mm-hmm! Very good. By the way, where's Nikos staying these days?"

Gorse shrugged. "Search me. He never even gave me a phone number. I'm just supposed to take the package up to a cabin in Maine, where I've been staying, and hand it over there."

"Is that all?" Q prodded. "What about that letter you were carrying—from Dracov?"

"Oh, that. Well, somebody named Dracov is supposed to contact me while I'm in London. I'm not sure why—he just wrote me out of a clear blue sky—but I'm hoping he may have some information about my father. Dad disappeared, you see, while he was in Europe at some scientific conference."

"So I've heard. And this information you will also pass on to Nikos, eh?"

"That's right. Of course I'm not supposed to mention that to Dracov."

"No, no. Of course not. Might spoil everything." After a whispered exchange with the psychologist, Q ended the interrogation. "Well, that's all, my boy. You can relax now."

Back in his office with the two TEEN agents, Q stoked up his pipe. "So far so good, eh? The picture begins to shape up more clearly."

"About as clear as mud to me, sir," said Chris.

"To begin with, it's obvious that Gorse is a TOAD dead man," Q said smugly.

Chris nodded. He knew that in the jargon of intelligence work, a "dead man" was a courier of absolutely dependable loyalty—someone who asked no questions and knew nothing about the purpose of his own mission. "But Gorse seems to believe he actually *is* me—and he was speaking under truth serum."

"Quite so. TOAD often employs a special type of dead man on delicate assignments. They'll offer protection to a wanted criminal like Gorse, then give him plastic surgery and brainwash him into total amnesia. The operation involves novocaine injected behind the eyeballs. It's like wiping the slate clean. After that, they can convince him he's anyone they choose."

"But why should they go to so much trouble to find out what Dracov knows about my father?"

"It's clearly an intercept job, designed to spoil some operation by the Dracov Network. In my opinion, it's probably less important than Gorse's main assignment—to pick up this mysterious package for Nikos."

"How so, sir?"

Q shrugged. "Merely from the way Gorse told it. Look at it this way. TOAD is sending a dead-man courier to London—someone who's tabbed for plastic surgery, anyhow. He can easily be made to look like you. So—why not? Let him be contacted by Dracov while he's there. Kill two birds with one stone."

Chris sighed. "Sounds reasonable. You noticed that password bit—about rare insects?"

"I did. Which reminds me—" Q stabbed another button and spoke into his intercom. "Lang? What about those hornets or whatever they are?"

"Not much to report, sir," a voice replied.

"Well, whatever you have, come up and report it!" Q bellowed.

Presently Lang, one of TEEN's staff scientists, arrived at the office. He was carrying one of the cages with a still-anesthetized hornet inside. Even Q appeared startled at the size of it.

"Nasty-looking brute! What is it?" he asked.

"We've no idea," Lang confessed. "Anatomically it's like an ordinary yellow jacket, but of course much larger. As far as I know, nothing so enormous has ever been reported."

"What about that ultrasonic gear?"

"Almost certainly the oscillator gave off the same frequency of ultrasound as the mating call of the female hornet. The three captured hornets are all males. They no doubt responded to this ultrasound and homed in on the source."

"Boiled down then," said Q, "you mean the ultrasonic oscillator was used to attract the hornets, as Kingston One here suspected?"

"Exactly."

After Lang left, Q paced the office, hands behind his back, bushy eyebrows knit in deep thought. "Our next move is clear," he said to

Chris. "You'll hop a plane immediately to London and carry out Gorse's double mission."

Chris gulped slightly. "In other words, sir, I'm to impersonate Gorse impersonating me?"

"Couldn't have put it better myself. You'll pick up, or do your best to pick up, the package for Nikos from Eli Lustig. It may give us an important clue to TOAD'S operation.

"Judging from his address, Lustig may be a jeweler, since Hatton Garden is the diamond Center of London. Try to lay hands on the package. Then wait to be contacted by Dracov and see what he says about your father."

"What about me, sir?" Geronimo asked. "Chris and I usually work as a team."

"Hm! You'd better go along. He might need a bit of support in case of trouble. You'll have to travel separately, of course, and stay away from each other—at least until after the pickup from Lustig."

The TEEN chief shot a glance at Chris. "You realize, British TOAD may have you under observation from the moment you arrive, so you must strictly avoid any contact with our London CIA station. You'll be completely on your own."

Chris nodded. "Understood."

"Of course," Q went on, "TOAD knows by now that their operation is fouled up. They may have found out Gorse was picked up at the airport, and British TOAD will certainly know that you're arriving on a later plane than Gorse planned to take."

"They might even suspect that Gorse was replaced," Chris said.

"Of course. The first thing they'll do is check Kingston U to see if you're still there."

"And find out—"

"That you're in jail." Q grinned smugly.

"Beg pardon, sir?"

"Well," Q explained, "Gorse will come in handy impersonating Chris Cool, who was jailed yesterday during a campus riot. We're already given the story to the press, and pictures will be taken in jail to follow it up while you're in London."

Chris smiled. "Very clever little scheme."

"You'll just have to play it by ear from now on," Q continued. "That's why we pick you brilliant young chaps for TEEN—able to think your way out of these tight spots, eh? At any rate, that's your assignment. Shall we get cracking?"

The boys rushed to Kingston by helicopter to pack their bags. Then they were flown back to Luxury Motors for their final briefing. Pomeroy, the fussy little technical genius of TEEN's "Department of Dirty Tricks," outfitted them each with the usual gimmickry for an overseas mission.

By four o'clock the next morning they were on their way to Kennedy International Airport in separate taxis.

5 · Hot Line

LONDON AIRPORT HAD been fogged in earlier, and planes were still stacked up waiting to land. Chris's jet finally came down and he joined the line of passengers trooping through Passport Control and Customs.

"Wonder if Gerry's in yet," he thought. The Apache had been booked on Pan American.

When Chris emerged onto the main floor of the terminal, he found the place besieged by a horde of screaming teen-age girls. The latest pop-singing sensation, it developed, was about to land. Meanwhile, helmeted bobbies were struggling to hold back the fans.

"Fat chance of spotting any TOAD agents in this bedlam," Chris thought. More than ever,

he missed his redskin buddy. Geronimo's Indian
radar was sharp enough to spot an enemy even
in a riot mob.

Outside the air terminal, Chris found a black,
slab-sided taxi and told the driver to take him
to the Thackeray Arms Hotel.

"Righto, guv'nor!"

Soon they were barreling over the elevated
motorway and the Great West Road toward "the
Big Smoke." A cheerful flow of cockney dialect
from the front seat gradually raised Chris's
spirits. He began to think the job might even be
fun.

London closed in around them with its
quaint, grimy Victorian buildings. They went
past Hyde Park Corner and drove up Piccadilly
into Jermyn Street. Chris paid the fare and
fumbled for a tip to the cabby while the hotel
doorman, in a coachman's hat and uniform, took
his luggage.

"Would seven shillings be about right?"

"That'd be lovely, guv."

Grinning, Chris walked into the lobby and
registered at the reception desk. "I believe I
have a reservation," he murmured.

"Yes indeed, sir. Five-four-four. Room all
ready and waiting!" The clerk snapped his fingers and a bellhop who had Chris's suitcase
walked over to the porter's desk for the key.

The chief porter spoke to Chris. "Mr. Cool?

You had a phone call just a few minutes ago."

"Oh? Who was it?"

"The man didn't leave his name, sir. But he said he'd ring back shortly."

Chris accompanied the bellhop into the elevator. He had a faintly uneasy feeling. Was Dracov already trying to contact him? Or had the caller been someone from the British branch of TOAD—or possibly Geronimo?

Inside 544, Chris flipped the rosy-cheeked bellhop a coin and waited until the boy had left. Then he stood thoughtfully for a moment, looking around the comfortable, old-fashioned room.

"Better check for a bug," Chris decided. The room might turn out to be "all ready and waiting" in more ways than one.

From his wallet, Chris took out what looked like a plastic credit card with raised lettering. Methodically he moved about the room, running the card over the walls and furniture. The faintest signal from a hidden transmitter would make the lettering on the card glow red.

But no glow appeared, even when he came to the telephone on the night table. Suddenly Chris turned pale as a horrible suspicion struck him.

"That phone call! The oldest trick in the book —a bomb!"

Grabbing the telephone cord, he yanked it loose from the wall box. Then he clamped the receiver in its cradle with one hand and turned the phone upside down. With a tool from his pocket kit, Chris unscrewed the base plate.

"Wow!" A neat-looking, lethal assembly was clamped inside the phone housing.

Chris's TEEN training had given him enough expertise in explosive devices to make out its workings. The bomb was designed to be armed by the ringing of the telephone. When the receiver was lifted, a secondary current was induced in the detonator circuit and—*boom!*

Perspiring nervously, Chris disconnected and disassembled the device.

"Now what do I do with the ruddy mess?" he wondered. He couldn't just drop it in the wastebasket, or even call the police bomb squad—not unless he cared to answer a number of awkward questions which might blow his masquerade sky-high.

The simplest solution seemed to be to carry the dangerous parts of the bomb down to the Thames River and give them the deep six. Chris carefully wrapped the detonator cap and the explosive cartridge in handkerchiefs and stuffed them into separate pockets. The bits of wire and other debris he stowed out of sight on a closet shelf.

He had just finished screwing the base plate back onto the telephone when he heard a knock.

"Who is it?"

"Hall porter, sir!"

Chris went to the door and opened it cautiously, one hand on his anesthetic pen.

"Sorry to trouble you, sir," said the porter, "but someone's calling you on the phone. The switchboard operator tried to ring your room but she says the line seems to be dead."

"Oh, really?" Chris faked an expression of surprise. "I'd better go see."

He walked over to the telephone. "Oh, oh! Look at that! The line's loose from the wall box."

"Blimey, how'd that happen?" said the porter. "We shall have to get it fixed straightaway. Meantime, you can tyke the call on my phone, sir, if you don't mind stepping down the hall."

They went down the hotel corridor to the porter's office, where an ironing board was set up with a pair of trousers on it. The porter took a wall phone off the hook, contacted the operator, and handed the instrument to Chris.

"Christopher Cool speaking."

"Yes. Here's your call, sir."

"Hello? . . . Hello!" There was silence, then a gentle click. Chris jiggled the hook for the operator. "Nobody answers."

"Oh, dear. I am sorry. I expect your party must have got tired waiting and hung up."

"Yes, I expect so," Chris said dryly. The TEEN agent asked for the reception desk. Chris explained to the clerk about his disconnected phone and requested a change of room.

"Of course, sir. Let me see. I can put you in five-four-nine."

Half an hour later Chris left the hotel and headed toward Piccadilly Circus. The second call had undoubtedly been intended to kill him when he lifted the receiver and triggered the booby trap.

But who had planned his death? It seemed unlikely that Dracov would lure him all the way to London just to kill him. And if TOAD was behind the plot, then Nikos must suspect the switch of couriers.

"Either he didn't check Kingston U," Chris mused, "or he just doesn't want to take any chances."

In any case, Chris realized, he was in a nasty spot. Whoever had arranged the booby trap would probably try again. And if Chris switched hotels, he might lose all chance of contacting Dracov and obtaining any clue to his father's fate.

The streets were swarming with homeward-bound office workers. Queues were lining up at the bus stops and snaking their way into the Piccadilly underground station. Red double-decker buses chugged through the London traffic, filling the air with petrol fumes.

Chris strolled down Regent Street, then via Pall Mall and Trafalgar Square to the river. On the Victoria Embankment along the Thames, he paused idly, glanced around to make sure no one was watching, and dropped the bomb parts into the water.

Aware that Londoners are late diners, Chris killed time sightseeing for the next two hours. He walked along the embankment and turned up Horse Guards Avenue to Whitehall, pausing to stare admiringly at the guardsman on sentry in his plumed helmet and shiny boots.

"Wonder how the Prime Minister's making out," Chris thought. On an impulse, he strode up the narrow, dead-end lane of Downing Street. A majestic, mustached bobby stood on duty in front of Number 10, the official residence.

"Greetings from America," said Chris. "And how's your Prime Minister these days?"

The bobby grinned back. "Best of 'ealth last time Oi saw him, young fellow!"

Chris walked on to Westminster Abbey, then crossed over to Westminster Hall and the Houses of Parliament topped by Big Ben.

It was going on eight o'clock when Chris finally took a table in a restaurant. The room was crowded and service was somewhat slow. He ordered from the menu, and presently the waiter brought him a bowl of turtle soup.

Chris started to dip his spoon, then stopped short. A large fly was floating on the broth!

"Hold it!" Chris exclaimed. "Bit of insect life here, I'm afraid."

The waiter clucked apologetically. "Most inexcusable, sir! Can't imagine how it got there. I'll bring a fresh bowl."

"Aha!" A woman's deep, hoarse voice spoke from a table on the left. "So you, too, are discovering the insect menace, young man!"

Chris turned in surprise. "I beg your pardon?"

The speaker was a large woman wearing a shabby tweed suit and a shapeless hat perched on a mass of brindle hair. Her piercing eyes stared at Chris through a gold lorgnette.

"The insect menace, young man—of which that fly in your soup is just a sample! Surely you're aware that the creatures threaten the very existence of mankind! A million species, breeding like mad, gradually taking over the whole earth!"

"Imagine that!" Chris murmured. He was evidently up against one of those typically dotty English dowagers he had read about.

"You realize, of course," the woman continued, "their biological efficiency far surpasses our own." She rattled off facts about bugs to prove her point.

Chris squirmed and coughed.

"As a matter of fact, I am organizing a society to cope with the problem. You might care to join one of these days." She handed Chris a card and added darkly, "The menace is far greater than you may suspect!"

The card read:

> AGATHA, DUCHESS OF SOHO
> Founder & Chairwoman
> Counter-Insect Association

Chris mumbled something politely and managed to turn away as the waiter brought another bowl of soup. For the rest of the meal, he carefully avoided looking around.

When he left the restaurant, Chris hailed a taxi and gave Lustig's address. It was two minutes after nine when the cab dropped him in Hatton Garden, the street of diamond merchants. Chris paid the driver and turned to study the three-story building.

On the ground floor was a shuttered jewelry store bearing a different number. But a doorway on the right, evidently leading upstairs, had a sign:

> ELI LUSTIG
> DIAMONDS BOUGHT & SOLD

Chris pressed the bell and heard it ringing inside. No one answered. He glanced up. The top-floor windows showed light and a shadow moved across one of the blinds. Chris rang the bell again.

It was answered by a shrill scream of terror!

6 · Watcher in the Dark

ANOTHER FEARFUL SHRIEK split the stillness!

Chris tried the door and found it locked, then glanced up and down the block. No one in sight. Without hesitating longer, he whipped a slender tool from his pocket and picked the lock.

R-r-ring! A burglar alarm erupted loudly as he pushed the door open! Chris was startled by the clanging. But a third, weaker scream halted his impulse to flee.

"Can't let somebody get murdered!" he thought and scrambled up the stairs. Chris rounded the second-floor landing, went past a darkened glass door which also bore the name Eli Lustig, and pressed on up the next flight.

On the third floor he came to another door,

this one wooden. It opened to his touch. Chris entered. Not a sound.

It was an office with a desk and file cabinets. The drawers had been ransacked and papers were scattered about.

In one wall of the office was an open doorway, leading to another lighted room. Chris ran on through and skidded to a gasping halt. It was a living room, with a thick Persian carpet and heavy mahogany furniture. Against the sofa lay a man who was bleeding.

Chris darted to his side. The victim, wizened and gray-haired, looked as if he had been attacked by some wild animal. His arms had been flung up to protect himself, but his sleeves had been ripped and both his face and arms were gashed with what looked like claw marks.

"Must be Lustig!" Chris guessed. He fumbled for signs of a pulse, then started bolt upright as his ear caught the noise of movements above the persistent ringing of the alarm.

Whoever, or whatever, had attacked Lustig must still be in the building!

"Somewhere in back!" Chris told himself as he strained to listen. He dashed through the apartment and found a door that opened on a rear stairway.

The next moment came a shrill police whistle from the street—confused sounds of people bursting in, trampling up the front stairs.

"Better leave!" Chris decided fast. "Fine time I'd have now, trying to explain what I'm doing here."

He plunged down the black stairway. A chill shot up his spine as he heard noises on the flight below. Someone else must be ducking out the same way—presumably Lustig's attacker!

"Be great to run into the creep!" Chris thought. "Especially in the dark!"

A door opened and slammed somewhere below. Chris continued his descent, trusting to luck not to lose his footing in the darkness. He found the back door and darted out into a narrow, twisting alley. Chris turned left and scuttled along through the alley.

Whang! He collided with a dustbin and knocked it over. Muttering with rage and pain, Chris hopped on one leg and rubbed his shin for a moment, then resumed his flight.

The alley connected with a street adjoining Hatton Garden. Chris slowed a bit, but kept to a brisk walking pace, trying to put as much distance as possible between himself and the scene of the crime.

Eventually he found his way to the Farringdon underground station, where he hastily studied the subway map before buying a ticket. In case someone might remember his face, Chris took a roundabout route on the Circle Line to Charing Cross. There he got off and walked through London's brightly lighted theater district, working back toward Piccadilly Circus.

When he finally reached his hotel, Chris glimpsed a figure lurking in a darkened doorway across the street. The doorman saluted with a cheery "Good evening, sir!" Chris returned the greeting. When he looked across the street again, the figure was no longer in sight.

Should he walk over and investigate? "Better not, with the doorman watching," Chris decided.

He got his key and went up in the lift to 549. Even though his room had been changed, it gave him no sense of security. "Not with that stakeout across the street," Chris thought.

He took a pen from his pocket and plucked off the cap of his infrared snooperscope. After unlocking the door cautiously, he scanned the darkened room through the scope but detected no sign of an intruder. The bathroom and closet were also empty.

Chris walked over to the window and peered out through the curtain.

"Still there!" The figure in the doorway had not only reappeared—he definitely seemed to be watching the hotel.

Chris drew the shade, then turned on the light, being careful not to show himself in the window as a target. "What about bugs and booby traps?" he wondered. "Better play it safe."

He checked over the room, bath, and closet but found nothing. At last he undressed and put out his shoes for the hotel boots to shine, switched off the light, and crawled into bed.

"Whew! I'm bushed!" Chris murmured to himself. No sleep the night before, except for his doze on the plane. Tomorrow would be soon enough to figure out what, if anything, he could do about his thwarted contact with Lustig and the package for Nikos.

Chris found himself too keyed up to fall asleep. As he stretched, trying to relax, he became aware of a faint, persistent buzzing.

"Hey! What's that?" Chris sat up tensely, then gave a sheepish grin in the darkness. "Just a fly. Must've come in through the open window. Boy, I'm really on edge. Have to watch that. No way for a cool-cat TEEN agent to act!"

Chris settled back on his pillow. Thoughts unreeled jerkily in his brain, like the twitching images of an old-fashioned nickelodeon movie. Flies. Insects. The book, *Behavior of Insects*, in Shenko's car. The giant hornets. The daffy dowager at the restaurant and her gabble about "the insect menace."

"Wow!" Chris came alert again as if he had been pinked with a hot electrode. Maybe that insect-menace jazz wasn't just silly chatter! "I've *really* been goofing off! Why didn't I get the connection before?"

Perhaps Agatha, Duchess of Soho, was a TOAD agent, who had been trying to slip him a message. Had she already been seated in the restaurant when he arrived? Or had she come in afterward and taken a table beside him? Chris wasn't sure. For all he knew, she might have shadowed him all the way from the hotel.

"Counter-Insect Association." Did that mean something? . . . CIA! Oh, oh! Was it possible she was an American agent, assigned to keep a helpful eye on the situation?

More buzzing, close to his nose this time. Chris brushed the fly away with an angry mutter and sat up abruptly. He was too disturbed now to put up with any more insect dive-bombing.

"Baby, you've had it!" Chris swung his legs out of bed and reached for the lamp switch.

Suddenly he stiffened. Down at floor level— reflecting back a faint glow of light from around the window shade—two small, beady eyes gleamed in the darkness!

Chris switched on the lamp. A rat! Instead of scurrying off, it crouched motionless, staring at him fixedly. Chris's flesh crawled.

"Don't just sit there, repulsive!" he muttered. "Go on, beat it!"

Still the rat refused to move.

Chris groped cautiously on the floor for his slipper, intending to throw it. The next instant, the rat attacked! Chris flung up his legs and rolled across the bed, catapulting himself to a standing position on the other side.

"Good grief! The thing must be rabid!"

Chris backed away hastily, just in time, as the rat darted under the bed toward him. Again he danced clear as it made several lunges. The thing was actually pursuing him!

Step by step, Chris waltzed his way toward the closet. In one lightning move, he yanked the anesthetic pen from his suit coat and zipped off a sleepy sliver. The rat flopped on its side.

Chris stared at it for a moment in sheer horror.

"Whew!" His heart was thumping and cold sweat was trickling down his sides.

"Baby, did someone plant you here? Or did you just crawl out of the woodwork?" He shot another sliver into the rodent's head to make sure it was dead, then wrapped it in tissue and dropped the rat into the wastebasket.

But the fly was still at it. *Buzz-z-z-z.* Chris got a towel, swatted the insect, and finally crawled back to bed. In two minutes he was asleep.

Hours later the shrill ringing of the telephone aroused him. He glanced at his watch as he groped for the phone. It was still early: 6:51.

"Hello—?"

"Choonday!"

"Geronimo!" Chris exclaimed. "What's up?"

"Plenty!" Geronimo spoke fast in Apache. "Have you seen the morning papers yet?"

"I'm not even out of bed!"

"Then get out pronto! Out of your hotel, too!"

"Why? What's wrong?"

"Eli Lustig's place was broken into last night," the Indian replied, "and Lustig was attacked."

"I know that, but—"

"He's in the hospital in bad shape. They don't know if he'll pull through. The joint was also burgled. Big haul of diamonds."

"What else?"

Geronimo hesitated for a moment.

"What else? Hold on tight, *choonday*. Your mug's plastered over the front page of every newspaper in London!"

7 · Fox and Hounds

"What?" Chris gulped. "How did that happen?"

"Lustig had secret cameras rigged to photograph intruders," Geronimo explained. "I take it you had to pick the lock to get in. Anyhow, you must have tripped one of the cameras because it snapped your picture. The police released it to the press."

"Rotten luck!"

"Someone there at the Thackeray Arms is bound to recognize you," Geronimo went on. "That's why I decided to risk calling. Better clear out fast, white eyes—and don't spare the horses!"

Chris needed no urging. "I'm on my way, redskin!" He hung up and leaped out of bed. As he flung on his clothes, Chris realized, "I sure can't go strolling out of here with my suitcase! Have to leave that behind."

Too bad. One or two tricky little gadgets of Pomeroy's were in the suitcase, but nothing important.

He froze suddenly at the sound of footsteps along the corridor. They stopped just outside his door! Chris's pulse skidded—was the law already about to close in?

There was a faint noise which Chris could not make out. Then the steps went on down the hall. Chris let out his breath in a sigh of relief.

He wasn't safe yet, though. Not with his friendly neighborhood booby-trapper still in business! "The guy could have planted one right outside my room," Chris told himself tensely.

He tiptoed to the door in his stocking feet. The steps halted again and there was a *clump*. Then more steps going away.

Puzzled, Chris eased the door open and peered out. A man in a white coat was wheeling a cart down the corridor. He stopped two rooms away to deposit a pair of freshly shined shoes.

It was the hotel boots who polished the guests' shoes during the night! As the man set the pair down, he noticed Chris.

"Morning sir!"

"Good morning." Grinning foolishly, Chris stooped to pick up his own gleaming loafers.

Then the boots did a double-take—took a sudden second glance, this time with a startled expression.

Chris withdrew hastily into his room and shut the door, his heart thumping. "Did that guy recognize me?"

He could hear the man's footsteps going down the corridor faster now. Then a slam. The service door at the end of the hall!

"Maybe he's rushing downstairs to tell the manager that he's spotted the guy pictured on the front pages of the newspapers!" Chris thought.

In an icy sweat, he jammed his feet into the loafers and pulled on his blazer. Then he slipped out into the hall. The shoe cart, still half-full, was standing near the door to the service stairs.

Which way down? "The stairs would be safer," Chris decided. "I could probably duck out the back way without going past the desk. On the other hand, I might run smack into the boots!"

Chris decided to use the lift and risk a bold exit. Turning left, he strode to the front hall. The elevator indicator pointed to ground floor. He took a deep breath and pressed the button.

Moments went by with no response. The car was still on the first floor. "What's going on down there?" Chris wondered uneasily.

He put out his finger to ring again, then stopped short as the indicator needle began swinging upward.

Could the police have been summoned this fast? It seemed unlikely. "But maybe the chief porter or someone else recognized my face before the boots did!" Chris realized suddenly.

His stomach churned at the thought. Acting on a blind impulse, Chris dashed down the hall toward the bend in the corridor away from his own room. He halted just around the corner as the lift stopped. He heard the door opening and people coming out. Their footsteps headed away—in the direction of 549.

Chris peeked cautiously. He saw the manager and a uniformed policeman! He waited until they were out of sight, then darted into the elevator and pressed the first-floor button. The door slid shut and the car descended.

Chris's pulse was a bit calmer by the time the lift reached the ground floor. As the door opened, he whipped a handkerchief to his nose.

Several people were moving about the lobby. The reception clerk was registering a guest, and at the porter's desk a bellhop and a girl employee were sorting the mail.

Chris walked boldly out of the lobby and past the doorman—the handkerchief still clutched to his face. "Morning," he mumbled huskily in response to the doorman's greeting.

His pace increased as he strode along the street. Traffic was already brisk on Piccadilly and a number of people were on their way to work in shops and offices. Chris headed for Piccadilly Circus, hurried down the steps into the underground station, and bought a ticket for Hammersmith, a distant suburban stop.

In two minutes he was on a tube train, rumbling westward under the streets of London. But instead of riding all the way to Hammersmith, Chris got off at the first stop, Green Park.

From the platform he made his way through the milling throng of commuters and along a sloping, white-tiled passageway toward the upper level. At a sign marked MEN'S WASHROOM he turned off.

Inside the lavatory was a separate cubicle containing several sinks, soap, and towels. "Sixpence, please," said the attendant, scarcely looking up from the racing news.

Chris gave him a coin and was admitted to the cubicle. He bent over a sink and hastily went to work as the attendant returned to his paper.

From an inside pocket, Chris pulled out a compact disguise kit. Hair dye applied with a brush changed him rapidly from blond to brunet. Small foam-rubber pads, stuffed inside his cheeks, strikingly altered the contour of his face. Dark glasses completed the change.

Chris glanced out the windows of the cubicle to make sure the attendant's nose was still buried in the racing news, then emerged and strode quickly out of the lavatory.

On the street once again, Chris relaxed for the first time since Geronimo's call. "At least I'm safe for a while," he said to himself.

But the thought was cold comfort as he mulled over the full extent of his plight.

As he walked along, Chris imagined what Q would say—that is, if he ever got a chance to see the old boy again in the next ten years.

"Scotland Yard will be watching for me at all airports, harbors, every way out of the country. And it's a cinch the American embassy won't be able to do me much good, except provide legal counsel."

There was always the odd chance, of course, that he might be able to lay hands on a fake passport, with Geronimo's help, and return to New York in disguise. But trying to buy a passport in the right quarters with a possible murder rap hanging over his head might be very chancy indeed. Meanwhile, his double mission in London was almost certainly washed up.

"Maybe I goofed last night by not staying put at Lustig's place and facing the—"

Chris broke off as a warning signal buzzed in his brain. Footsteps behind him. Faint but steady.

Chris stopped at the next pedestrian crossing and turned to face the traffic. From the corner of his eye, he noted the person who had been following him—a little man in a bowler hat and striped pants, umbrella over one arm, head bent reading a folded newspaper. Typical London type.

"Where have I seen him before?" Chris wondered, starting across the street. Suddenly he knew the answer. He had seen the man on the underground platform, back at Piccadilly Circus!

Chris paused momentarily on the corner as if to get his bearings. Bowler Hat was following him across the street. No doubt about it. If the man had been on the platform at Piccadilly Circus, then he must definitely have hung around waiting at Green Park station until Chris emerged from the washroom. Which in turn meant that he had probably tailed Chris all the way from the hotel!

"The morning relief for the hotel stakeout," Chris deduced.

The TEEN agent grinned wickedly as his pulse stirred with excitement. A little action coming up, perhaps. Better than glooming, anyhow!

Chris started off briskly. Again he heard the faint patter behind him. In the next block Chris came to a telephone call box. He went inside, consulted a directory, and rang Geronimo's hotel. Through the glass, he could see Bowler Hat pausing to look at some "gents' shirtings" in a shopwindow.

Presently Geronimo came on the line.

"This is your old buddy, the white pony soldier," Chris told him in Apache.

"What's up, Fearless Leader?"

"Got out of the Thackeray Arms okay, but now I'm being tailed. How about setting up an ambush at the pass?"

The two boys laid their plans rapidly.

Then Chris hung up and emerged from the call box, whistling softly. Geronimo's hotel was located just a few blocks ahead, near Hyde Park. Chris walked toward it steadily.

Presently he sighted his Indian pal in the distance, coming toward him. The two boys passed with no sign of recognition. Chris kept going until he had counted to fifty, then suddenly whirled around.

Bowler Hat was still on his tail. By now Geronimo had passed him, too. Chris strode quickly toward the little man, whose face contorted in alarm. He turned to flee—only to find Geronimo waiting.

Bowler Hat sensed his danger instantly. He raised his umbrella and pointed it straight at Geronimo. Chris heard a faint report like a cork popping as a puff of smoke issued from the tip!

8 · A Count of Nine

As THE UMBRELLA weapon fired, Geronimo was already doing an aiki whirl. The puff of smoke went past his shoulder, and an instant later the Indian came at his man low and hard, arms akimbo.

They collided with a grunt and Bowler Hat crashed backward with the Apache on top of him. Chris reached them in a dozen steps and yanked the umbrella from Bowler Hat. Then he and Geronimo helped the man to his feet.

"Play it peaceful, friend," Chris warned. "This brolly's pointed right at you!"

Several passers-by had turned to glance at the trio but walked on without stopping, apparently assuming that there had been an accidental sidewalk collision.

"Let's get moving," Chris said. "Toward the park. Take his arm, Gerry."

The Apache assented with a grin. Geronimo and Bowler Hat went first. Chris followed a pace or so behind, swinging the umbrella dapperly so that now and then its tip brushed the back of the little man's coat.

"Shall we start talking?" Chris said. "Don't bother turning your head, please."

"Talk about what?" Bowler Hat snarled.

"Who sent you? Why were you tailing me?"

There was silence as they walked along.

"Come on," Chris urged. "Start beating the gums together, there's a good chap. Bit of a bore, I know, but let's not make it any more painful than necessary."

Bowler Hat sneered, "You two yobbos don't frighten me. You wouldn't dare try anything on a public street—and I hardly think you'd turn me over to the coppers, now would you?"

"Quite right," Chris said pleasantly. "But then I hardly think you'll keep up this stubborn attitude very long, either."

He spoke rapidly to Geronimo in Apache.

"Is that Pig Latin?" asked Bowler Hat.

"No—trouble. For you, old boy."

They came to Hyde Park Corner and crossed over. Entering the park, Geronimo steered the little man toward the Serpentine—a long, placid pond fringed with trees. At this early hour the park was almost empty and the greenery glistened with dew in the morning sunshine.

Chris tagged along behind the pair as they headed down along the brink of the pond. Presently the trees and shrubs hid them from view of the other park strollers.

Chris's manner now became more businesslike.

"Fun's over, old chap. Talk fast and clearly, and don't try our patience any further. You know better than I do what will happen if this brolly goes off."

"You can't get away with this!" Bowler Hat gritted.

"You'll never know," Chris bluffed their prisoner. "After your body plops into the Serpentine, who'll be the wiser?"

Bowler Hat still held out.

"I'll count to nine," Chris warned. "You'll have that long to change your mind. On ten—*poof!* . . . One, two, three, four, five, six, seven, eight, nine—"

"*Wait!*" The word came out in a stifled half-scream. "I'll talk! Just—just take it easy."

Geronimo eased his grip.

"What's your name?" Chris asked.

"Peveny. Alf Peveny."

"Who sent you?"

"Dracov."

"Well, well!" Chris's eyebrows rose. "What were your orders?"

"Shadow you anywhere you went. Don't lose you. Report your movements."

"You were staked out at the hotel?"

"That's right. Came on at six. Followed you to Piccadilly Circus, then by underground to Green Park. That disguise bit didn't fool me."

"I resent the slur on my professional ability," said Chris. "Still, it all works out neatly in the end. So happens I'm eager to meet Mr. Dracov. Tell us about him."

"Can't. Never laid eyes on him. I'm just an agent for the network, paid by the job. 'S' truth, so help me! Strike me dead if it's not! I just get my orders by phone, and money in an envelope through the mail slot on the day after."

"All right, we believe you," Chris said. "Ease off, Gerry. And let's have a peek at his wallet."

Geronimo frisked his prisoner with one hand. He found a switchblade knife which he dropped into the pond, and passed a wallet to Chris.

It contained a driver's license and other identification made out to Alfred E. Peveny. His street address was in Southwark, a dingy residential area across the Thames. Chris copied the information, which included a telephone number, then handed back the wallet.

"Okay. We'll let you go, chum. On one condition."

"What's that?"

"That you arrange a meeting between me and Dracov as soon as possible. My name's Christopher Cool, in case you didn't know."

"I did. And I think I can fix you up." Bowler Hat frowned as he rubbed his wrist. "There's a chap at a pub I can contact."

"Can we reach you at that number in your wallet?" Chris asked.

"Righto. Make it three o'clock."

"Fair enough. And don't let us down. I've snapped your picture with my lapel camera, and a copy will go to Scotland Yard, with a full account, if there's any hanky-panky."

"Don't worry. I deal fair and square." Bowler Hat sniffed and looked insulted. "What about my umbrella, by the way?"

"Sorry. It's entirely too dangerous to be carried about on a public street—especially within range of us. Just toddle along, old boy."

The two TEEN agents watched him walk off through the park.

"He looks naked without that thing hanging on his arm," Geronimo remarked.

"So let him buy a raincoat," said Chris. He triggered off the five remaining cartridges before dropping the umbrella into the Serpentine.

The boys went to a restaurant for breakfast, and then spent the rest of the morning and early afternoon sightseeing.

At three o'clock Chris telephoned Peveny's number. A voice which he recognized as the little man's answered.

"Yes?"

"Cool calling. What's the drill?"

"British Museum. Rosetta stone. Five sharp."

Chris heard a receiver click down. He hung up and reported the result to Geronimo.

The Apache grunted. "Very neat—for Dracov. He has a complete description of you, but you don't even know what to look for. His game all the way."

Chris gave a wry shrug. "What did you expect? You have a better suggestion perhaps?"

"Yes. Quit this whole TEEN racket and go home to the reservation. Failing that, we have two hours to kill."

"Let's go back to your hotel. My dogs are barking."

At the hotel the boys stretched out for a short nap—Chris on the bed, Geronimo in a chair with his feet up on the radiator. At four o'clock the Apache ordered tea sent up to the room, and finally they started out by taxi for the British Museum.

En route, Geronimo cast several wary glances out the back window. "Not sure, but I think a car's following us."

To play safe, it was agreed that when they reached the British Museum, Geronimo would wait outside and signal an alarm over his wrist-watch communicator in case of trouble.

The taxi drove into the faded elegance of the Bloomsbury district and dropped them outside the imposing gray building. Chris paid off the cabby and they walked in through the gateway, past the small, crowded car park to the porticoed front entrance.

"So long, *choonday*," Geronimo muttered. He planted himself on one of the stone benches of the portico.

Chris went on inside to the marble foyer. A guard directed him left, past the Publications Counter and through the Assyrian Transept into the Egyptian Sculpture Gallery.

The transept was flanked by brooding stone lions with wings and human heads. Chris strolled on into the gallery—a long, narrow room with busts of pharaohs and other Egyptian pieces. A few visitors were wandering around.

In the center of the room on a lighted, glass-topped pedestal was the famous Rosetta stone— a tablet bearing three forms of writing, which had first enabled scholars to decode Egyptian hieroglyphics. Chris studied it casually.

"Hm! At least I can read two of them," he thought, scanning the Greek and demotic Egyptian.

Chris looked at his watch. Exactly five o'clock. "Wonder how long I'll have to wait."

He glanced around at the visitors. An elderly gentleman leaning on a cane. A tall RAF officer with a bushy "zoom duster" mustache. A nanny with two small children. A pair of giggly schoolgirls. None looked too promising.

Chris stiffened alertly as his wrist watch suddenly gave a buzz. Gerry's alarm signal! But he couldn't answer it here without attracting attention.

Chris turned and headed back into the Assyrian Transept, which seemed deserted at the moment. Just then two men came through the doorway from the foyer. They wore dark suits and had a tough, quiet look about them. They walked straight toward him.

Chris's heart thudded and his hand streaked to the inside pocket of his blazer where the anesthetic pen nestled cozily.

"Don't try anything foolish!" the tallest of the two men snapped. His hand flipped open a wallet to display his identification. "Scotland Yard Flying Squad. Are you Christopher Cool?"

Chris nodded, trying to keep his voice steady. "I am."

"I should like you to come along with us, please, for questioning in connection with a burglary in Hatton Garden and an assault on a man named Eli Lustig!"

9 · Night Shift

THE DETECTIVES MOVED into place on each side of Chris. "Now then, we suggest that you come along quietly."

"Who's arguing?" Chris murmured. It all seemed so reasonable and well-mannered that he would have felt like a boor to object.

As they came outside, Chris glanced around for Geronimo. The Apache was nowhere in sight!

A small black car was parked in the street. Chris was shepherded into the back seat and one of the two plainclothesmen climbed in with him. The other took the wheel and radioed Central Division before starting off.

"Where to now?" Chris inquired. "Scotland Yard? Wormwood Scrubs?"

"Tottenham Court Road Station first, since we picked you up in their territory."

At the station Chris was led in and shown to the desk sergeant. Then out to the car again and a drive eastward into Theobald's Road.

They pulled up before the Holborn Police Station, a low, modern-looking building. "The crime was committed in this division, so you'll be questioned here," Chris was told.

Inside, one of the Yard men spoke to a desk sergeant. "This is the lad who's wanted for that job in Hatton Garden last night. We picked him up at the British Museum."

The sergeant eyed Chris keenly and reported over the phone. "Okay, take him upstairs. The super will see him."

The two Flying Squad men escorted Chris to a second-floor room. There he waited in silence until two other men came in. One, burly, with iron-gray hair, was introduced as Detective Chief Superintendent Hart. His companion was a younger, hard-faced detective.

"Sit down," said the superintendent, then held out his hand toward Chris. "Passport?"

Chris handed it over.

Hart flipped the pages and studied the passport photo. "Remove those glasses, please."

Chris did so.

"Will that hair dye come off?"

"I hope so," said Chris.

Superintendent Hart turned to his assistant. "Take him to the washroom."

Chris was taken to a lavatory, where the detective pointed to a washbasin, soap, and paper towels. "Go to it."

As he bent over the basin and soaped his hair, Chris spat out the foam-rubber pads inside his cheeks. Fat lot of good his disguise had done him!

Back in the interrogation room, Superintendent Hart surveyed the results approvingly. "Ah, that's better. So you're Christopher Cool?"

"That's right."

"Where were you last night shortly after nine o'clock?"

"At 98 Hatton Garden."

"Well! So you admit that, do you?"

Chris permitted himself a wry grin. "Wouldn't do me much good to deny it, I imagine."

"Very little indeed, seeing that your picture was snapped when you broke in," Hart said sharply. "What was your business there?"

"A friend in America asked me to call on Mr. Lustig while I was in London."

"What friend?"

Chris pretended to hesitate. "I prefer to keep

his name out of it, if you don't mind. He had nothing to do with what happened."

"Suppose you tell us what happened."

"I got there soon after nine, rang the bell, and heard several screams inside. There was no one else in sight on the block, so I broke in. I was afraid Lustig was being murdered."

"A remarkably expert job of breaking and entering," Hart remarked with heavy sarcasm.

"I've studied locksmithing," Chris said.

"Humph! Go on."

"Well, the burglar alarm startled me, but I rushed upstairs anyhow, thinking Lustig needed help. There he was—all clawed up and not moving. I didn't even know if he was still alive. Then I heard a police whistle and people bursting in and—well, I guess I got the wind up a bit. I knew I was in a spot, so I ducked out."

Hart's assistant and the two Scotland Yard men joined in the grilling. Chris fielded their questions as well as he could. The superintendent scowled and rubbed a large hand over his thinning hair. "You expect us to believe this story, son?"

Chris shrugged.

Hart rose to his feet with a ponderous sigh. "In that case, there's no more to be said. Your embassy has already been notified. No doubt you'll be hearing from them in due course."

To his assistant, Hart added, "Book him."

The detective took Chris to the charge room, where a policeman was seated at a typewriter.

"Christopher Cool, I hereby charge you with burglary and grievous bodily harm against the person of one Eli Lustig, diamond merchant, on his premises at 98 Hatton Garden," the detective intoned, "and I warn you that anything you say may be taken down and used as evidence against you. Do you wish to make a statement?"

Chris shook his head.

"Yes or no?"

"No."

The policeman at the desk typed up a form which both the detective and Chris had to sign.

"What happens now?" Chris asked.

"You'll be detained here overnight, and to-morrow morning you'll be arraigned at Clerken-well Magistrate's Court. Probably the American embassy will have legal counsel on hand for your defense. If not, the court will appoint one."

Chris was fingerprinted and his pockets emp-tied. Then he was locked in a neat, yellow-tiled cell with a stout oak door and one high, barred window. The door was opened soon afterward by the turnkey who brought him dinner.

Chris ate the steak-and-kidney pie with small appetite. He had hit rock bottom, all right. The fate feared by all secret agents—under arrest in a foreign country, with no hope that his own service could or would stir a finger to aid him.

After all, he had been fairly warned of the risks when TEEN first recruited him.

"Boy, this mission has been a disaster from start to finish," Chris reflected.

Could they actually convict him? No diamonds could be traced to his possession. Of course the police could claim that he must have worked with a confederate. Probably it was just as well that Gerry had cut out when the police arrived!

Chris lay back on his bunk and pictured himself in the dock, with bewigged judge and lawyers debating his fate. . . . "And how do you find the defendant?" . . . The judge was putting on a black skullcap. . . . Gradually Chris dozed off.

A light blinked on in the cell and Chris surged up out of his deep sleep. He blinked at two figures near his bunk—a plainclothes detective and a uniformed constable.

"On your feet, please," said the detective.

"What's this all about?"

"We're taking you to the Royal Free Hospital in Gray's Inn Road to be X-rayed."

"X-rayed?" Chris stared at him.

"You may have swallowed some of the diamonds to keep them from being found on you. Now then, come along."

Chris was taken below to the station garage and put into a police car with his two escorts.

It was after midnight. The luminous hands on Chris's watch dial pointed to 1:27.

The car turned right along Theobald's Road.

"You aren't taking me to any hospital," Chris said. "Gray's Inn Road is the other way."

His escorts said nothing.

Chris finally got his bearings as the car passed Marble Arch. They were heading west into Bayswater Road.

At last the police car pulled over outside a small office building in a seedy neighborhood. Chris was taken inside, up in a lift, then into an unmarked suite of offices.

A tall, lean man in shirtsleeves, with a sardonic face and a vaguely military air, sat at a battered desk. Nearby sat Geronimo.

"*Hondaal, choonday,*" the Apache murmured. "Hi, pal." His copper-skinned face was as expressionless as ever.

"Here's Cool, sir," said the detective.

The man at the desk nodded a curt "Thank you." As the door closed, he gestured Chris to a chair. "Have a pew. My name is Folliott. And you're Christopher Cool—otherwise known as Kingston One."

"I beg your pardon?"

Folliott chuckled. "No need to beat around the bush. We know you're an American agent."

"That so?"

"Oh, quite. After the hotel chaps identified

you from the newspaper photo, Scotland Yard cabled the FBI for information on you. The FBI routed the query to the CIA, which passed it on to your particular unit. They decided to throw their cards on the table and seek our cooperation. Hands across the sea and all that."

"Sounds like a spy-story plot," Chris remarked.

"Yes, doesn't it? The CIA people here in London briefed us on your whole mission. I—"

He broke off as one of the three telephones on his desk rang. "Ah! Your chief was to call us at oh-two-hundred hours. May be him, I expect."

Folliott lifted the left phone. "Oh, yes. Q is it?" He talked a while, then looked at Chris. "Your chief wants to speak to you."

Chris took the phone gingerly. It was Q's voice all right. The TEEN chief proceeded to identify himself with the current top-secret password for hazardous voice transmissions.

"Got yourself into a bit of a jam, did you, Kingston One?" No doubt about it—this was Q.

"I—er—ran into complications," Chris said.

"Mm-hm. You can tell me all about it when you get back. Meanwhile, go ahead and work with the Limeys. They're not a bad lot. Quite good at this sort of thing, really—in spite of a few security leaks as big as the Lincoln Tunnel."

Chris glanced at Folliott, aware that the call was probably being taped. Q must know it, too, and was probably trying to slip in a few quick rabbit punches to cover his own red face over the foul-up.

"Well, that's all," Q ended. "Unless you have any questions."

"No, sir. Understood." Chris hung up and explained to Geronimo. Then he turned back to Folliott. "I take it the CIA gave you the name of Gerry's hotel."

"That's right. The Flying Squad got there as you were boarding a taxi and trailed you to the museum. One of our men who accompanied them took your partner in charge separately."

Chris felt a bit better. At least his disguise hadn't been so bad. They had spotted him merely from the fact that he was with Gerry.

"If you knew about our mission," he asked Folliott, "why all that rigmarole about charging me at Holborn Police Station?"

"Well, we haven't exactly blared the news all through the Force, you know," Folliott replied. "Have to keep up a bit of cover. Actually, word will be given out to the papers that you escaped from custody after being taken to the hospital."

Chris nodded. "Okay. Let's get down to business. What can you tell us about Eli Lustig?"

"For one thing, we believe him to be a top-echelon director of TOAD's British branch. Also we know who Lustig's other visitor was."

"Oh? How so?"

"Fingerprints. The Yard men picked up a

clear set of dabs belonging to a known Dracov agent."

"Who is he?" Geronimo asked.

"When I say 'known,' I mean he's known to belong to the Dracov Network," Folliott explained. "Actually we have nothing else on him. His prints were first obtained off some microfilm that had passed through Network hands."

"But no burglar alarm had been tripped before I got there," Chris said thoughtfully.

"Right. So Lustig must have let him in. For some reason, maybe a quarrel, the visit ended with an attack on Lustig. Then the Dracov man fled when you set off the alarm. There may have been *two* Dracov men, by the way—one cracking the safe while the other assaulted Lustig."

Chris frowned. "What about those gashes on Lustig? They were like claw marks—almost as if he was attacked by a wild animal."

Folliott drew a deep breath and leaned back in his chair, toying with a pencil. "That's an interesting question. I must now tell you something very odd—which has so far been kept secret from the British public.

"A man—Chinese—was found recently in a wooded area of Kent, not far from London. He'd been horribly gashed and chewed. The work of some savage animal, it appeared. He was out of his mind with terror. Completely insane. He's been in the hospital since, hovering near death, and we haven't been able to get anything out of him. And our best zoologists still can't tell from the marks what sort of animal attacked him."

Chris and Geronimo exchanged startled looks.

"What about the Chinese?" Geronimo asked. "No clues to his identity?"

Folliott nodded. "Yes. Through various Intelligence sources, we finally discovered who he is. Wong Hsiu—a brilliant biochemist. He's rumored to have slipped out of China via Hong Kong . . . with a formula for some new secret terror weapon of biological warfare."

Chris gave a low whistle. "What's he doing over here?"

"Another good question. The danger immediately arises that the weapon may be about to be turned loose on England. So, because of the potential threat to the whole population, the mystery was turned over to our department."

"You're in the Secret Service, I assume," Chris said. "MI-5?"

Folliott grinned coldly. "No, old chap, we're a rather special unit, set up to cope with extraordinary threats to national safety—and now that you two are taking the Queen's shilling, you'll be members of our little group. We're called the Department of Danger."

10 · The Contact Problem

THE DEPARTMENT OF Danger! There was something about the words that sent a faint chill down Chris's spine.

Again Geronimo's eyes met Chris's. "You thinking the same thing I'm thinking, *choonday?*"

"The package I was to pick up for Nikos?"

The Apache nodded. "TOAD's always in the market for useful terror gimmicks. Maybe the package had something to do with this biological warfare weapon."

"Hm! A most disturbing thought," said Folliott with a frown.

"There also is the possibility," Chris suggested, "that the Dracov agent or agents may have snatched the package from Lustig last night."

80

"An equally disturbing thought, since Dracov might well sell the formula to one of our enemies." Folliott rubbed his lantern jaw worriedly. "I should say, Kingston One, that our best bet is for you to carry on with your mission in spite of what has happened."

"You mean, try to make contact with Dracov?"

"Or British TOAD."

"As a matter of fact," Chris said dryly, "I was about to meet Dracov himself at the British Museum just before the Flying Squad picked me up."

"How very vexing!" Folliott chuckled. "Still, these little bungles do occur. One must just press forward, chin up, and shoulder to the wheel. Tell me—have any attempts been made on your life since you arrived in London?"

"Yes. At least one, maybe two." Chris told about the booby-trapped telephone and his encounter with the rat.

"In that case, I fear TOAD may already be trying to kill you."

"You mean, because their operation's fouled up?" Chris queried.

"Exactly—even before you left the States, I'm told. Several underlings captured. Their courier nabbed at Kennedy Airport. And why did the FBI let him go? Bit fishy, that's how it's apt to strike TOAD. For all they know, he's been subverted. Safer to kill the chap and take no chances.

After all, their dead-men couriers are expendable."

"Could be," Chris agreed.

"However, that's a risk you'll have to take," Folliott said. "The important thing is to make contact first, then try to talk away their suspicions."

"Great." Chris's voice was a trifle tart. "And how do you propose I do that—make contact, I mean—now that Lustig's out of action?"

"Hm! Well, now. Let's put ourselves in Gorse's place and think what he might do in just this situation. For one thing, I should think he might phone Nikos back in the States and ask for new orders."

Chris shook his head. "No dice. Gorse told us under truth serum that he had no phone number or address for contacting Nikos. He was simply supposed to deliver the package to a cabin in Maine."

"Then he'd be in just as tight a spot as you were."

"Are," Chris corrected dryly.

Folliott drummed his fingers on the desk. "In that case, I would suggest two possible moves. First, there's a discotheque here in London called Queenie's which we strongly suspect is a hangout and meeting place for TOAD members. You might go there and see if any TOAD agent contacts you."

"It's not likely Gorse would know the place," Chris said.

"True again. But if he had mingled with the London underworld while he was dodging the police, he might have heard a few whispers about it. Or, second," Folliott went on, "he might put a carefully worded ad in the Personal Column of the *Herald* on the chance that someone in TOAD would notice it."

Picking up a pencil, Folliott thought a while, then dashed off the following message which he handed to Chris:

> *Mr. Diamond. Advice on rare insects needed urgently by friend of Nikos.*

Chris read the message and nodded approvingly, then passed it on to Geronimo. "Very good. It'll need a phone number to call, of course, or some other way to get in touch."

"Right," said Folliott. "Which brings up the question of where you're to stay in the meantime. A hotel won't do, I'm afraid, even if you wear a disguise, since they're bound to check on your passport. Some cheap lodging house would be more natural, where the landlady doesn't bother with that sort of thing. Soon as you find a place, notify me of your phone number and I'll attend to the *Herald* notice."

On a sudden afterthought Chris asked Folliott about the Duchess of Soho. "She wouldn't be an enemy agent, by any chance? Or is she just some con artist or an eccentric?"

"New one on me," Folliott said. "Don't believe I've ever heard of her. However, I'll check with Scotland Yard."

Belatedly, Chris realized that he might have asked Q the same question.

Geronimo was driven back to his hotel, while Chris slept until morning on a makeshift cot in the Department of Danger offices. Next morning he found that his suitcase and other belongings had been brought by a Flying Squad car.

After breakfasting on coffee and buns, Chris reapplied his disguise and sauntered off into the London scene, clutching his suitcase. He bought a morning newspaper and found a table in a restaurant where he could study the rooming-house ads.

The paper carried a brief front-page item headed HATTON GARDEN ATTACKER ESCAPES FROM HOSPITAL. Chris grinned wryly and was about to leaf through the pages in search of the classified advertisements.

Suddenly his eye fell on another news story. It was headed VICIOUS MONSTER REPORTED AT LARGE IN KENT!

11 · The Face Behind the Gun

THERE WAS A startled expression on Chris's face as he read the newspaper account. It told how a farmer in Kent, named Arthur Simpson, had been attacked the night before by some vicious, unknown creature.

Simpson was almost incoherent when he reached the nearest house and could give only a confused description of the animal that had attacked him in the darkness. He said it was "about the size of a hog, with needle-sharp teeth and clawlike feet."

He was taken to Wardley Hospital and is still under sedation. Doctors have described his wounds as severe.

Rumors of a savage beast at large in the area have been circulating for the past ten days. Simpson appears to be the first human to encounter the creature, but numerous attacks on sheep and other livestock have been reported.

"Not quite the first human," Chris thought grimly. "Wong Hsiu beat him to it!"

The news story went on to suggest likely explanations. An escaped circus or zoo animal. A wild dog. Even a large hawk or eagle.

"May be," Chris mused. "But what about Eli Lustig? Had a hawk flown down his chimney?"

On the other hand, Lustig's wounds had not been nearly so bad as Simpson's or Wong Hsiu's. Besides, he had heard footsteps at the jeweler's house.

Thinking about Lustig reminded Chris of Dracov. He finished his coffee and picked out one or two likely rooming-house ads, then went to a phone booth in a corner of the restaurant and dialed Bowler Hat's number. A woman's voice answered.

"May I speak to Mr. Peveny, please?" Chris asked.

"Sorry. 'E's no longer 'ere."

"You mean he's gone out for the day?"

"I mean 'e checked out last night. Packed up an' left. This is 'is landlydy speakin'."

"What about a forwarding address?"

"Sorry. Didn't leave none. An' Oi've no idea 'ow to get in touch."

Chris fumed in frustration. "But this is terribly

urgent," he pleaded. "Almost a matter of life and death! Can't you think of any way that I might reach him? Any place? Or any friends who might know?"

"We-e-eell . . ." The voice softened somewhat as the usual cockney good nature came through. "There was one thing Oi noticed when Oi cleaned up 'is room. Please 'ang on a sec."

Presently she returned to the phone. "Oi did find this scrap o' paper with a name an' address on it. Musgrave, Gunsmith. Name of a shop, Oi expect." She read off an address in St. James's Street.

Chris copied down the information. "Thanks. I certainly appreciate that."

Chris paid his bill and decided to go to the gunsmith shop as soon as he had rented a room. He caught an underground train and got off at Sloane Square in Chelsea—an arty, Bohemian district somewhat like New York's Greenwich Village.

Heading into King's Road, which led off from the square, Chris eyed the passers-by with interest. Young men with beards, side whiskers, hair longer than Geronimo's. Girls in short skirts and colorful "kinky" stockings.

Chris asked a youth for directions to the addresses given in the rooming-house ads. Following the direction which led him through a warren of side streets, he finally came to a tall, narrow, gray Victorian tenement house. A sharp-eyed but loutish-looking boy answered the bell. "Wotcha want?"

"I understand you've a room to let here."

"'Ave to speak to me Mum about that." With a grudging air, he allowed Chris to enter the musty foyer, hung with red-plush drapes.

Presently the landlady appeared, a small, sparrowlike woman. Chris introduced himself as Charles Cass and learned that her name was Mrs. Snite.

She glanced at Chris's dark sunglasses, then at his suitcase. "You an artist?"

"No, ma'am. A student."

Mrs. Snite sniffed. "Very well. Follow me." Her son tagged along behind as they started up the staircase. Mrs. Snite stopped him with a cuff on the ear. "Wasn't talkin' to you, Bert!"

On the third floor she showed Chris a tiny bed-sitting room at the end of the hall and named the weekly rent. "In advance, please."

Chris started to count out the money, then paused. "By the way, is there a phone here?"

"First-floor hall."

He asked for the number and jotted it down, explaining, "I'm trying to locate a friend in London, so I may get one or two phone messages. If the caller doesn't know me by name, he may just ask for 'a friend of Nikos.'"

Mrs. Snite nodded and sniffed as she went out.

Chris unpacked and settled into his room. Then he left the house and headed back to King's Road. From a telephone call box, he rang Folliott and gave him the lodging-house phone number to insert in the Personal Column ad.

"It'll be in the afternoon *Herald*," Folliott promised.

"Short notice, isn't it?"

"Don't worry about that. We're the Department of Danger, old boy."

"By the way," Chris added, "did you see that story about the Kent monster in the morning news?"

"I did. Matter of fact, it happened quite close to where our Chinese friend was found."

After his conversation with Folliott, Chris called Geronimo. He gave him his new address and phone number, and they made arrangements to meet later at Trafalgar Square. Then he took an underground train to Piccadilly Circus and walked down Piccadilly to St. James's.

Musgrave's gunsmith shop had the same plush, aristocratic air as the famous London gentlemen's clubs whose rooms overlooked the street nearby. The name was spelled out in brass letters above the shop.

Chris pushed open the door and went inside, his footsteps sinking into deep-pile carpeting. Racks of rifles and shotguns with polished walnut stocks, some with gleaming damascened barrels, lined the walls. Above were mounted big-game heads and framed sporting prints.

Two customers were being waited on. One was a slim elegant young man who was saying something about a grouse shoot in Scotland.

The other, a thick-set, ruddy-faced fellow with a bristly military mustache, was trying out a rifle. He clamped the gunstock to his shoulder and the magazine to his cheek as he squinted through the sight.

Another clerk came out of the back room to greet Chris. "May I help you, sir?"

"I hope so. I'm trying to locate a Mr. Peveny—Alfred E. Peveny."

The military man's rifle swung around sharply and Chris found himself staring down the business end. Its bore looked big enough for an elephant gun, and a pair of beady eyes stared at Chris from the other end.

Chris stared back and the rifle muzzle dropped abruptly.

"Oh! Sorry, my dear chap! Didn't mean to startle you."

"You didn't," Chris said pleasantly.

Harrumph! The ruddy-faced gunner cleared his throat. "In point of fact, you startled *me*, sir. That name—Peveny. Alfred Peveny. I have a very dear friend by that name. I wonder if it might be the same chap."

"I don't know. What's your friend like?"

"Little. Prim. Dresses like a city clerk. Hardly ever see him without an umbrella."

"That's the man," said Chris. "Can you tell me how to get in touch with him?"

"I might. Haven't seen Alf in a few years, but I dare say I can run him to earth for you if your business is urgent."

"It is," Chris replied. "Very urgent."

The ruddy-faced man reached inside his tweed jacket, drew a small leather case from his tattersall-checked vest, and plucked out a card, which he handed to Chris. It read:

MARMADUKE BUTTRAM, o.b.e.
Lt. Col. (ret.) H. M. Coldstream Guards

"How do you do, sir?" said Chris. "I haven't a card myself, but my name is Charles Cass. I'm just visiting over here."

"Enjoying your stay, I trust. Now then, is there some way I can reach you?"

Chris jotted down his phone number on a slip of paper borrowed from the clerk, who said, "Then you're all taken care of, sir?"

"Yes, thank you. Unless *you* know Mr. Peveny?"

"Hm! I don't recall the name, sir. Did you—er—expect to find him on the staff?"

"I'm not really sure," said Chris. "I was just given to understand that he might be known here at Musgrave's."

"Dear me . . . I don't believe so. . . . But I shall be glad to check our list of customers."

"Don't bother," Colonel Buttram said heartily. "Poor old Alf wouldn't know one end of a fowling piece from the other. I can assure you he's no patron of Musgrave's."

After a parting handclasp, Chris walked up Pall Mall to Trafalgar Square, where he met Geronimo near the tall column topped by the figure of Admiral Nelson.

The boys spent the next two hours in the nearby National Gallery. Then they treated themselves to a long lunch.

When they came out of the restaurant, Chris bought an afternoon London *Herald*. The "Mr. Diamond" notice had been inserted in the Personal Column.

"So far so good," said Chris. "Let's go back to my rooming house and see what develops."

The boys were just settling down in Chris's room when young Bert Snite rapped on the door.

"Call fer ya," he announced.

Chris hurried to the telephone in the first-floor hall. "Hello?"

"You're a friend of Nikos?" said the man on the other end of the line.

"That's right. From New York."

"Good. I have the information you want."

12 · A Bottle of Fireflies

CHRIS'S HEART LEAPED. Someone was snapping at the bait.

"Where are you?" the man went on. "I'll come and get you."

Chris's brain did a microsecond calculation of the risks. If Gorse were in this situation he would certainly sniff the air a few times before poking his nose out. "I think I prefer to meet in some *public* place. You can bring the package there."

The man hesitated before replying, "There's been a slight hitch about the package. We'll have to talk it over."

"All right. Let's say tomorrow in front of

Buckingham Palace. The Changing of the Guard. I'll be standing near the fence, just right of the main gate. Whom will I look for?"

"You won't," the man said coldly. "I'll look for you."

"Suit yourself. I'll be wearing dark glasses. Just reverse the password procedure." Chris purposely refrained from mentioning the rare insect bit.

"Good enough." The receiver clicked, and Chris walked back through the hall toward the staircase.

Entering his third-floor room, Chris found Geronimo lounging by the window, looking down through the curtains at the street. He told the Apache about the call.

"Think it was the McCoy, *choonday?*" Geronimo asked. "Or someone trying to deal himself in?"

Chris shrugged. "Don't know. Just have to wait and see if I get any more calls. If this guy *was* a TOAD man, there's no telling what he has in mind—maybe a hole between the eyes."

The boys killed time playing rummy. An hour later Chris was summoned to the phone again.

"Hello?"

"This is *not* Mr. Diamond speaking." The voice was deep and hoarse, but unmistakably female.

"No, I gathered that," said Chris. His pulse

had just taken a quick skid. Unless his ear was
playing tricks, the caller was Agatha, Duchess
of Soho!

"It happens I am a devoted reader of the Personal Column," she went on. "My eye was
caught at once by your mention of insects. *Insects!* My good man, I wonder if you realize the
terrible danger which these vermin pose to us
all."

"I'm not sure that I do," Chris said.

"Ah! But I and my fellow workers *are* aware,
fully aware, of the insect peril. Our Counter-
Insect Association has been expressly set up to
alert the world and give advice on such matters.
By the way," she added querulously, "your
voice sounds familiar, young man. Have we met
before?"

"It's possible," Chris evaded. "Anyhow, I'll be
happy to talk to you. You may have just the advice I need. What's the address of your organization?"

"We have no formal address, but I am Agatha,
Duchess of Soho. You can find me tomorrow
afternoon at three o'clock at the Speaker's Corner
in Hyde Park. I frequently devote time to public
speaking, in my effort to arouse the British
people to the insect crisis."

"I'll be there," Chris promised.

He went back upstairs thoughtfully. What was
the old girl? A kook? An agent? It had to be

more than just coincidence running up against
her twice in a city the size of London!

Chris stopped short as he went into his
room. Geronimo was poised watchfully near the
window, and it was obvious his Apache radar
was at work.

"What's wrong?" Chris murmured.

"Not sure. Maybe nothing, but a car's been
parked down near the end of the block ever since
you took that first call. And no one has gotten in
or out of it."

Chris strode to the window. This side of the
building looked out over a low stucco house,
giving a partial view of the street that ran in
front of Mrs. Snite's rooming house.

The car was a dark-gray Humber. A man was
at the wheel, but it was impossible to see his
features.

Geronimo moved away from the window.
"Think I'll sashay down there and have a look-
see."

"No fire arrows, please," Chris said uneasily.
He watched at the window until his buddy came
into view on the street below. The Indian walked
casually toward the parked car.

Geronimo was still a few yards from the Humber when the car started with a sudden roar and
a billowing blast of blue exhaust smoke. Geronimo staggered and whirled around to avoid the
smoke, then pitched forward on his face.

Chris rushed out of his room and down the staircase. When he reached the street, it was empty of cars and pedestrians. Most of the smoke had lifted and only a faint bluish haze remained. Geronimo was getting to his feet. His necktie had been ripped open and was plastered over his nose and mouth to form a TEEN emergency gas mask.

Chris rushed to him. "You all right, Gerry?"

"Okay. Little woozy, that's all. I managed to get the mask on before I inhaled too much of that goof gas." Geronimo berated himself grumpily in Apache as he smoothed out his tie. "I sure walked into that one! And I was so busy keeping my eye on that guy in the car, I didn't even get his license number."

"What'd he look like?"

"Tall, I think. And dark. Didn't turn his face. He was watching the rear-view mirror."

"Never mind," Chris said. "At least we're forewarned that my pueblo has been spotted."

The boys walked a few blocks to clear Geronimo's head and then came back. They had just entered the foyer when the hall telephone rang. Mrs. Snite's head popped out of her room as Chris strode to answer it.

"Hello?"

"Cool?"

"Who is this speaking?" Chris asked.

"Peveny. Alf Peveny."

"Oh, I see. Colonel Buttram gave you my number, did he?"

"Buttram?" Peveny sounded startled.

"Yes. I went looking for you at Musgrave's and ran into him there," Chris explained. "He said you were an old friend."

There was a brief, strained silence. "I know the gent," Peveny said at last.

"But that's not how you got my number?"

"No. The Dracov Network traced you from that notice in the *Herald*."

"Well, well. Very clever," Chris said cautiously. "How'd they manage that?"

"No trick to that, me lad. 'Mr. Diamond'—who else but Lustig? He was a TOAD director, and that 'friend of Nikos' bit spelled TOAD, right enough. And it was a dead cert *you'd* be needin' urgent advice with every copper in London lookin' for you. That's why the Network was watchin' the Personal Column."

"I see." Suddenly Chris sensed himself treading in a deadly morass of danger and suspicion. If he ever did contact Dracov, he would now have to explain his involvement with TOAD. "No doubt your control knows about me getting picked up at the British Museum?"

"They do. And they also read in the paper about you escapin' from the hospital. Now then, do you still want to meet Dracov?"

"Definitely!"

"Where and how soon?" Peveny asked.

"Sooner the better." Chris hesitated. He had planned to go to Queenie's discotheque around ten. Perhaps he could meet the Dracov man nearby later.

"Eleven-thirty tonight," he told the man and gave a café on Shepherd Market as their meeting place.

"Righto." Peveny hung up.

Two hours later the TEEN agents started out from the lodging house on foot. They kept an alert eye but no one appeared to be following them.

In King's Road they stopped in a restaurant. While they were eating, Geronimo asked, "You intend to keep your disguise on at the discotheque, *choonday?*"

"Have to," Chris replied. "Someone might spot me and call a bobby."

"What about TOAD? If you want *them* to spot you, you'll have to risk showing your own face."

Chris scowled as he sipped his coffee. "You have a point there. Maybe I should at least ditch the dark glasses." Suddenly he broke into a grin. "Tell you what. I'll carry a lighted sign, too."

Chris added a generous tip when they paid the bill and asked the waiter for an empty bottle from the kitchen.

Leaving the restaurant, the boys hailed a taxi

and got off at Hyde Park Corner. Chris led the
way into the park, now shrouded in soft, moon-
lit darkness.

"I hope you know what you're doing," said
Geronimo. "I don't."

"You'll see."

As Chris had hoped, a few fireflies could be
seen glimmering here and there among the greenery. He caught several, put them in the bottle,
and corked it.

The Apache stared at him. "That's your lighted
sign?"

Chris grinned. "Why not? London's full of ec-
centrics. Who's going to object if I carry around
a few pet insects?"

The boys walked to Shepherd Market in May-
fair, an alley-like maze of shops and cafés. Here
they found the entrance to Queenie's.

After signing the guest register, they were
ushered down a flight of steps into a crowded,
dimly lighted room. The walls were decorated
with rainbow-colored op art designs and the
room throbbed with a deafening blare of music
from the stereo speakers. Couples were writhing
and gyrating on the dance floor.

The two boys were shown to one of the low
tables. Chris removed his dark glasses and set
out his bottle of fireflies in plain sight. The twin-
kling insects drew several joking remarks from
people at the surrounding tables.

Chris merely smiled in response.

A blonde girl in a fluorescent-pink dress approached. She was wearing purple-lensed, rhinestone-studded harlequin glasses, which gave her face the appearance of a huge insect. On her dress was a flowerlike pin.

"I say! Would you care to dance?" she asked Chris.

"My pleasure!" He bounced up from his chair and they moved out to join the other dancers.

The girl's inviting smile changed to a tense, wary expression. "You're Chris Cool, aren't you?" she asked abruptly.

Chris nodded, his eyes watchful.

"Don't you realize you're in terrible danger here!" It was a statement, not a question.

Chris felt a faint chill of fear, but his voice remained casual. "Oh? From whom?"

The smile came back on the girl's lips—this time cold and menacing. "From me," she replied sweetly. "This pin on my dress is a miniature poison-dart gun—and it's aimed right at you!"

13 · Redheaded Surprise

THE GIRL'S THREAT caught Chris by surprise. He stiffened for an instant, but quickly picked up the beat of the dancing again.

"Sorry, you'll have to aim higher," he murmured. "I'm wearing bulletproof underwear. Sort of a nylon-and-steel-mesh body stocking."

The blonde stared at Chris evidently not sure whether he meant the remark to be taken seriously. Finally she relaxed with a giggle.

"You know, I like you," she confided. "I think Nikos has very good taste in picking couriers."

Couples all around them were dancing in a sort of stupefied ecstasy as the din of music beat against their ears.

102

"Ah! Then you know all about Nikos, do you?" Chris inquired.

"Of course. He's top man in Yank TOAD. I'm TOAD dolly 324 in British Wing, by the way."

"Name?"

"Pamela."

"Very nice. Always did like that name."

Pamela dimpled. "Thanks. Chris isn't bad either. . . . By the way, who's that with you?"

"Gerry? He's an American college boy I ran into. In a Chelsea pub. He's an Indian—Red Indian, that is."

"Does he know the coppers are after you?"

"Uh-huh." Chris nodded. "He's letting me hide out in his room till the heat's off."

"He seems to be doing all right," Pamela observed. Chris looked around, to see Geronimo dancing with a redhead who was also wearing harlequin "insect" glasses.

Chris did a double-take as the redhead's face came into better view. It couldn't be! But it was —Spice Carter, coed TEEN agent from Vassar.

The music stopped and Chris started back to his table with Pamela. Geronimo and Spice joined them.

Spice had helped the Kingston duo on two previous cases, filed under the code names *X Marks the Spy* and *Mission: Moonfire*.

"Nice going, Gerry," Chris said. "Shall we do the honors?"

The redhead extended her hand casually across the table without waiting for Geronimo to introduce her. "Lay five on me, boy. I'm Spice Carter, Main Line deb from dear old Philly and all that jazz, getting my final polish in Europe."

Chris beamed back as he squeezed her fingers. "All you need is one of those long Auntie Mame cigarette holders, honey, and you're ready for the big time. My name's Charles Cass and this is Pamela."

Spice tilted an eyebrow and looked the English girl over as if she were a lab specimen on a glass slide. "Pamela what?"

"Just Pamela, dear."

"How very quaint. And that pin you're wearing—where'd you pick it up? In Portobello Road?"

"A gift from the Queen, dahling."

Chris cleared his throat. "And her boy friend, Pamela, is Geronimo Johnson."

The British girl beamed. "Both from the same reservation, I presume." She turned to Spice again. "This 'Philly' you speak of is somewhere out in your Great West, isn't it?"

"West of the Hudson, quite right. Your expertise in geography fully matches your stunning appearance."

Music exploded again from the stereo speakers. Spice gave Chris a dazzling smile. "You're cute, Charles. Shall we dance?"

Pamela shot her a look of daggers, which Chris deflected with a faintly apologetic shrug before accompanying Spice out on the dance floor.

Face to face, the two TEEN agents began swinging to the wild beat.

Chris grinned. "To coin a phrase, What's a nice girl like you doing in a place like this?"

"Ask Q. He shipped me off to London this morning on about two hours' notice. And your friend Folliott informed me I might find you two here at Queenie's."

Chris briefed Spice hastily, but stopped short as he saw Pamela approaching them.

"May I cut in, dahling?" she asked Spice. "He's a poor thing, but mine own."

"Do, please." Stifling a yawn with her fingertips, Spice left the dance floor.

"Such picturesque friends you have," said Pamela. "Are all American birds like her?"

"Not all. Just the Main Line debs."

Pamela's face went coldly serious. "Let's drop the gay chit-chat, shall we? You realize that British TOAD has you marked for the kill?"

Chris did a comical shoulder-shrug.

"It's no joke, laddie boy! American TOAD alerted our London HQ that you were intercepted at Kennedy before take-off. The CIA might have persuaded you to work for them, and we prefer to take no chances!"

"I rather assumed as much," Chris replied,

"since they've already tried to do me in twice." But he was relieved. At least TOAD didn't seem to take him for the real Chris Cool. Q's scheme had worked. He looked at Pamela. "Just for the record, the CIA never even tried to work on me."

"If you say so—but I wouldn't bank too much on your chances of convincing London HQ."

"But I've already arranged a contact over the phone," Chris said. "For tomorrow."

"Probably setting you up," Pamela retorted.

"Aren't you taking a bit of a risk in telling me all this?"

"Putting my neck on the chopping block, but I'd like to see you live."

"Then what do you advise?"

Pamela danced for a while without replying. "You know Madame Macabre's Wax Museum? Be there tomorrow around five o'clock?"

"I'll be there."

The music stopped and they returned to the table. Spice and Geronimo were gone! Chris's eyes roved keenly about the dimly lighted room but could see no sign of either.

"Seems we've been abandoned to our fate," he remarked.

"I expect I can bear up," said Pamela. "One final word of advice. You're a very hot item. TOAD has an underworld dragnet out for you all over London, and this discotheque happens to be a favorite TOAD haunt, as you've no doubt heard. I shouldn't hang around too long, if I were you. And lie low when you leave here."

"Understood."

The music resumed. "Must go now," said Pamela. "Cheery-bye." She moved away in the swirl of dancers and disappeared through a door at the back of the room.

Chris felt uneasy. What had happened to Spice and Gerry? Had some TOAD agent quietly got the drop on them? Not likely—or else why would Chris himself have been left undisturbed? Or had the TOAD agent assumed Pamela was taking care of him?

Ten minutes ticked past slowly. Wherever Geronimo and Spice had gone, it seemed they were not coming back.

Chris rose abruptly and strode up the staircase, past the cloakroom and the desk where he had registered.

"Good night, sir. Hope you enjoyed yourself."

"Fun galore," Chris said. "By the way, that fellow I came with—the one with long dark locks, did he leave here with a red-haired girl?"

"Um, yes, I believe they did," the host said vaguely. "To tell the truth, though, I can't say I noticed them in particular. Other guests coming in and registering, you know—keeps one busy."

"Yes, I'm sure. Well, good night."

Chris unlatched the antique wooden door that

looked as if it had survived from the days of the first Queen Elizabeth, and walked out.

The café was only a few blocks away. As Chris opened the door, something hard pressed against his side.

"No fast moves, please," said a voice on his left. "I tend to be frightfully nervous on the trigger."

Chris glanced out of the corner of his eye and saw a tall, black-haired man with a bushy, up-twirled mustache. A memory clicked. "I do declare! The RAF officer at the British Museum!"

"Bang on!" the man confirmed. His mustache lifted in a toothy, sinister chuckle. "Well, old fruit, you wanted to meet Dracov—and that's exactly where we're going!"

14 · Bombs Away!

THE MAN'S RIGHT hand was out of sight in his coat pocket, clutching the weapon he had used to prod Chris.

"Delighted you showed up," the TEEN agent said coolly. "I'm eager to meet Mr. Dracov."

"Splendid! I can see we'll get on like a house afire!" The man with the mustache chuckled again. "Ringay's my name, by the way—Wing Commander Ringay. Now then, if you'll kindly start walking ahead of me—"

He broke off as a taxi rumbled into the crowded passageway, and blocked their route.

"Hold it, laddie!" Ringay's voice hardened.

The taxi disgorged two couples. As one of the

men paid the driver, the first girl who had got out looked around and said in an unmistakably American voice, "And where are we going now?"

"Right this way, please!" Chris spoke up brightly.

He whirled around, stepping away from Ringay, and gestured toward the door. Grinning, the four people passed single file between Chris and his captor.

As the couples disappeared inside, Chris stood with his left hand jammed in his blazer pocket. Something was poking out against the cloth. It was aimed straight at Ringay.

"Sort of a double-checkmate, eh?" Chris smiled back at the Dracov man's baffled scowl.

"None of your silly tricks, Cool. I know that's only your finger in your pocket!"

"Really?" Chris stepped closer until they were face to face.

For a moment Ringay hesitated, then reached out his left hand to feel the American youth's pocket.

At that instant Chris belted him in the short ribs!

The blow spun Ringay around and sent him tottering backward. Chris followed with an upward kick that hooked his foe's legs and dumped him on the pavement. Ringay's hand had jerked out of his pocket to break his fall.

Chris trod on his wrist and pulled a small automatic from his paralyzed grasp.

"Okay. On your feet, chum."

Fuming with helpless rage, Ringay got up. Chris, meanwhile, ejected the clip of shells from the magazine and tossed the gun away.

"No need for ordnance on a friendly little social call. Shall we proceed?"

Ringay brushed himself off and chafed his hurt wrist. "Bad enough, these monkey tricks," he said reproachfully. "Did you have to step down quite so hard?"

"Only way, I'm afraid, when someone's toying with dangerous firearms." Side by side, they sauntered down the alley.

"That uniform you were wearing at the museum," Chris remarked, "and the Wing Commander jazz—are you really in the RAF?"

"Was once. Just a supply officer, actually," Ringay confided. "Got cashiered for embezzling mess funds. But the uniform does look dashing, don't you think? And this mustache?" He gave it a fond twirl and chuckled. "Tell the truth, I never did like planes. I can hardly tell the tail of a Spitfire from the nose."

His car, a Vauxhall, was parked near the end of the passage. Chris got into the front seat and Ringay slid behind the wheel. The Dracov man keyed the ignition, swung the car around in reverse, then started forward. As they came out of Shepherd Market into Curzon Street, Chris heard him gasp.

Ringay gunned the engine and the Vauxhall shot left. At the same instant, a big black Bentley zoomed out from the curb on their right and rammed them amidships!

With a crash of crumpling metal, the Vauxhall heeled over slightly, then jolted back on four wheels again, but its engine was stalled.

The impact had knocked Ringay forward, banging his head against the windshield. His forehead was dripping blood and his right shoulder seemed to be pinned between the caved-in door panel and the steering column.

"They've pranged us, old boy!" he gasped. "It's the TOAD bunch! Better clear out!"

Chris, unhurt except for a small bump on the temple, saw a sinister-looking goon climbing out of the Bentley. Another sat poised watchfully behind the wheel. Two other cars had braked to a halt on the street. People were streaming toward them. Somewhere in the background a police whistle shrilled.

Chris made a lightning choice. Bursting out of the car, he yelled, "Quick! Get an ambulance, someone!" and took off at a run with the sinister-looking man after him.

He dashed down Curzon Street among the startled onlookers, then snaked off on a zigzag

course through the adjoining side streets. By
now he had lost his pursuer.

Several blocks away he finally slowed down.
"Oh, brother! . . . Now what?"

Chris paused in a darkened doorway, twirled
the stem of his wrist watch to Transmit, and
gave it a tug. This would produce a sharp buzzing signal on Geronimo's or Spice's watch if
either were within radio range.

No response.

Chris signaled again. "Kingston One calling
redskin and redhead! . . . Come in, please!"

Still no answer. Their silence was even more
alarming than their disappearance.

Should he go back to the rooming house?

Chris decided to play the situation by ear.
"I'll go back at least long enough to get my suitcase and find out if I've had any more phone
messages," he decided. "Then maybe I'd better
head for Gerry's hotel and wait around there. I
can always stash the bag at a railway station."

Chris took the underground to Sloane Square
and walked the rest of the way. As he approached
Mrs. Snite's rooming house, he slowed down
cautiously. The street appeared empty. Chris
circled the whole block but saw no sign of a stakeout.

The windows of the gray Victorian tenement
house were dark. Chris let himself in the front
door. The dimly lighted hall was wrapped in

silence. He climbed the two steep flights of stairs. On the third floor he walked softly to his room.

Chris was about to insert his key in the lock when he froze suddenly. A ticking noise was coming from inside the room.

Tick-tock . . . tick-tock . . . tick-tock . . .

Beads of perspiration stood out on Chris's forehead. It couldn't be an alarm clock—he had none. Somebody must have slipped in and planted the bomb while he was out!

"How do I get inside to disarm it?" Chris wondered. "Opening the door might trigger it!"

On the other hand, the ticking seemed to indicate an ordinary time bomb, rather than a booby-trap arrangement. "Not that that's any better," Chris realized. "If the thing goes off, it may kill everybody in the house!"

What time would the detonating device have been set for? Midnight? He'd have to do something—and fast—but what? Should he risk a booby trap and open the door? His hand holding the key moved back toward the lock, then withdrew gingerly again.

"There's more than my own life at stake!" Chris thought. "I'll have to rouse everybody and get them out of here!"

What a mess! But there was no other way out. No other *safe* way, at any rate.

"Better wake the landlady first," Chris decided, "and have her call the police!"

He turned and dashed back downstairs to Mrs. Snite's apartment. Sounds of nasal snoring came from within.

Chris rapped on the door. The snoring continued. He rapped several more times. At last the door opened. Young Bert Snite peered out.

"Yeah? . . . Wotcha want?"

"Wake your mother, please! I must speak to her at once!"

"Mum's asleep."

"Well, wake her up!" Chris exclaimed, his voice cracking. "Come on! Look alive, kid!"

Bert stared at him, but finally withdrew into the apartment. The snoring ceased with an explosive gasp. Presently Mrs. Snite appeared, in a bathrobe and hair curlers.

"Yes?" She frowned suspiciously.

Chris explained in frantic haste. "I think there's a bomb in my room! It may go off at any time! You'll have to get everyone out of the house! And call the police!"

"A bomb?"

"Yes! I can hear it ticking!"

Mrs. Snite gave him a withering look. "That ayn't no bomb—it's an alarm clock. I seen you didn't 'ave none, an' we 'ad an extra, so I put it in your room."

Chris slowly deflated, like a punctured balloon. "Oh—an—an alarm clock, eh?"

Mrs. Snite nodded, her lips pursed severely. Chris could see Bert grinning behind her.

The TEEN agent apologized, red-faced and sheepish, and went back up to the third floor. It was one of life's darkest moments.

Chris stopped at the end of the hall and inserted his key in the lock. He put his hand to the knob and opened the door.

Boom! A deafening explosion shattered the night stillness!

15 · A Suspicious Character

CHRIS STOOD STOCK-STILL, waiting for his pulse to calm. His heart was thudding like a triphammer and his legs felt rubbery. But at least he was still in one piece!

An acrid smell of gunpowder wafted from his room. Doors were opening down the hall, lights were flashing on, footsteps were pounding up the stairs.

"Nah then, wot's all this?" . . . "A bomb!" . . . "Wot's goin' on up 'ere?" . . . "Anyone killed?" Voices clamored frantically at Chris.

He collected his wits and turned to cope with the pajamed, night-robed roomers. Apparently the whole household had been roused.

"I'm afraid I don't know yet what happened,"

117

he told them. "I just opened my door and—
boom!"

Chris's brain was clicking at top speed now.
Had the bomb been a dud, or what? "Better
stay back till I see what's what," he cautioned
the people clustering around him.

They fell back gingerly. Chris went into his
room and pressed the light switch. Then he
looked on the other side of the door—and
the answer became clear. Two wires led to a pair
of small copper strips taped at the door crack.
When the door was opened, the strips had
brushed together and closed a circuit.

At the other end, the wires had been connected to a dry-cell battery—one of them by a
loop of fine wire, which no doubt had been
threaded through a king-size firecracker. The
fine wire, now charred and parted, had glowed
red-hot from the current and sparked the explosion. Shreds of the firecracker littered the floor.

"Just a practical joke, I guess," Chris announced.

Mrs. Snite appeared through the crowd. Her
sparrowlike face was white with outrage. "Queer
sort of joke, I'd call it!" she said sharply.

Chris shrugged as he saw Bert sniggering behind her. "Depends on your sense of humor. I
wonder who'd have firecrackers around here."

"*Firecrackers?*" Mrs. Snite's beady eyes suddenly blazed with suspicion.

"That's right," said Chris. "Somebody rigged one to explode from an electric spark as I opened up." He pointed behind the door.

Mrs. Snite rounded wrathfully on her son. "Bert Snite, you sneakin', ungryteful wretch!"

The wretch quailed under her tongue-lashing. His sly snigger changed to a shrill whine. "It was on'y a joke, Mum!"

"Joke, is it? I'll give you somethin' to joke about!"

Chris said hastily, "I'm sure he didn't mean any harm, Mrs. Snite. Quite clever, really, being able to rig a circuit like that!"

"Y-y-you 'eard the gent, Mum! I di'n't mean no 'arm!"

"Well, I do!" Mrs. Snite said as she cuffed him on the ear. Bert fled down the hall, pursued by his mother.

Chris cleared his throat uncomfortably and as the onlookers dispersed he closed the door.

"Whew!" Chris realized he was drenched in cold sweat. Switching off the light, he flopped wearily on the bed.

"I'll wait till the house is quiet again," he decided, "then freshen up with a shower and clear out."

Gradually silence settled over the household. Chris stripped to his shorts and put on a bathrobe. With a towel tucked under his arm, he went to the bathroom down the hall.

Ten minutes later he was toweling himself briskly and feeling more cheerful. In shorts and robe again, he switched off the light and went over to raise the window blind so the steamy atmosphere might clear a bit faster.

Suddenly Chris stiffened to alertness. Looking down over the roof of the house next door, he could see a tall figure walking slowly along the street. Chris drew back out of sight behind the window curtain to watch.

The man stopped near a parked car, pulled something from his pocket—apparently a notebook—and began writing. He paused and glanced up at the lodging house. The man was not close enough to a street lamp to be clearly visible, but he was mustached and had a bandage over his forehead.

Ringay!

"It must be him!" Chris thought. "Maybe it's still not too late to meet Dracov tonight!"

But the man was now climbing into his car. Was there still time to stop him?

Chris dashed out of the bathroom and down the two flights of stairs. Even if he was wrong and the man wasn't Ringay, it would do no harm to have his license number traced.

As Chris burst out of the house, the car was just starting up. It zoomed off before he was half-way to the curb.

"Rats!" The exclamation was barely off Chris's

lips when he heard the front door swing shut and the latch click.

"Oh, no! And my key's in the room!"

Another fine mess. Now what to do? Chris cringed at the prospect of rousing Mrs. Snite again after the "bomb" scare.

"Maybe I can pick the lock," he thought, then asked himself wryly, "With what?"

Chris groped in the pockets of his bathrobe. Empty. Naturally. In desperation, he began scanning the pavement and the tiny flower-bed patch around Mrs. Snite's front steps.

"Ah! A bent nail!" Chris saw its glint in the glow of light from the nearest street lamp. As he picked it up, he heard a faint roll of thunder. The sky was overcast and starless.

Chris went up to the front door and was about to insert the nail when he saw a figure coming along the street. It was a helmeted bobby, twirling his truncheon.

As the officer approached, Chris turned away from the door again.

"Evening, Constable. Not much breeze stirring tonight, eh?"

The policeman replied, "Hm," looking at Chris's bare shanks and sandaled feet beneath the skimpy bathrobe.

Chris smiled back foolishly. "Couldn't sleep. Had to come out for a breath of night air."

The constable nodded. "Wouldn't stay out

too long if I was you, sir. May come on to rain soon, I shouldn't wonder." He touched his stick to his helmet and passed on.

"Whew!" Well, at least the coast was clear now. Chris turned back to the front door and hastily went to work on the lock again. No luck!

Suddenly there was a blinding flash of lightning, followed by a cannonade of thunder. Next moment the rain came down in gusty sheets!

Chris gave up in despair and rang the doorbell. "I might as well get it over with," he thought grimly.

Several minutes and three rings later a light went on. The landlady peered out at him from a window. By this time Chris was drenched.

Mrs. Snite opened the door and looked him up and down. "Well!" she sniffed. "May I ask what you're doing out at this hour of the night, in a rainstorm, in that condition, Mr. Cass?"

Chris maneuvered himself inside and floundered out a feeble explanation as the landlady's eyes regarded him coldly.

"That's as may be, young man," she said when he had finished. "I asked if you was an artist when you came, an' you said No. Now then, I operate a respectable lodging house an' 'ave seen quite enough. First a ticking bomb in your room, an' now this! I shall expect you to leave first thing in the morning. Your rent will be returned—one night's lodging deducted!"

Clutching her sleazy pink robe, Mrs. Snite stalked back to her room and slammed the door.

There hardly seemed much point in going out to roam the streets in stormy weather. Chris napped until daybreak. Then he dressed, packed his suitcase, and crept out of the house. The rain was over.

From Sloane Square, he went by underground to Victoria Station, where he retired to a lonely corner bench in the waiting room. Masking himself behind an open newspaper, he tried buzzing Geronimo on his wrist-watch communicator.

The Apache answered, and a moment later Spice's voice chimed in from her own hotel.

"Where did you two disappear to last night?" Chris asked a trifle tartly.

"Spice thought she spotted a suspicious character," Geronimo replied. "Some fellow who'd been on the same flight with her coming over."

"Well, you must admit it did seem a bit too much of a coincidence," Spice added.

"Anyhow, we followed him from Queenie's and then tailed him on the underground all the way out to the London boondocks. False alarm I fear, *choonday*."

The underground. So that was why his radio call had got no response, Chris realized.

"What about you, K One?" Spice inquired.

"Long story. Let's have breakfast and I'll fill you in on my sad tale."

An hour later all three were tucking away bacon and eggs at a restaurant, while Chris related his night's adventures.

"So what's our next move, Fearless Leader?" Geronimo asked.

"Try making contact with TOAD at the Changing of the Guard," Chris said thoughtfully. "If that doesn't pan out, there's always the dear old Duchess of Soho in Hyde Park. And then Pamela at the Wax Museum at five."

Spice giggled maliciously. "Chamber of horrors, I presume?"

Chris shrugged. "I thought she was rather cute, myself."

Geronimo grunted and put down his coffee cup.

"Excuse me for interrupting, kiddies, but do you think this Changing of the Guard thing is safe? If what that Pamela squaw told you is on the level, TOAD may be setting you up for a poison dart or something."

"As dear old Folliott would say, that's a risk I'll have to take," Chris said dryly. "But let's see if we can't figure out some way to reduce the hazards."

The three discussed it for a while. Then Chris telephoned the Department of Danger and filled Folliott in on their plans for the day.

At eleven-twenty Chris descended from a taxi near Buckingham Palace. Tourists and other spectators were already collecting in front of the iron fence around the palace courtyard.

Chris mingled with the sightseers. Inside the yard, a pair of red-coated guards were pacing back and forth in front of the sentry boxes, stamping their boots smartly at each about-face.

Chris glanced about casually. A number of sightseers were clustered around the steps of the Victoria Memorial across the street, and among them his keen eyes picked out Spice. Geronimo was nowhere in sight. But he was lurking about some place, Chris knew . . . and so were a sprinkling of Folliott's security agents. Not to mention the usual bobbies and policewomen.

Presently, amid a great bawling of orders by sergeants major, the old guard began forming up inside the courtyard.

Meanwhile, where was TOAD? Somewhere in the crowd, at that very moment, an agent might be—

From a distance came a thump of drums and the scream of bagpipes. Down the Mall and past the Memorial came the Scots Guards, kilted pipers in the lead, skirling out "The Road to the Isles."

Chris's eyes strayed momentarily from the blaze of color. It was then that he spotted the TOAD executioner!

16 · House of Horrors

THE MAN WAS perched high on one of the statues of the Victoria Memorial, clutching a camera to his face as if about to snap a picture. But he wasn't photographing the pipers or red-coated Guardsmen—the lens was aimed straight at Chris!

Even as the TEEN agent swung around to scan the crowd across the street, he had seen the lens shift slightly to keep him in focus. And the cameraman was unmistakably the same sinister TOAD thug who had climbed out of the black Bentley the night before!

It was over in a split second. Chris dropped to the ground and heard a metallic *ping!*

A glittering steel needle had struck one of the

blackened bars of the tall, iron-grille fence around the palace courtyard!

In flinging himself to the pavement, Chris had collided with several spectators. There were angry mutters—which changed instantly to expressions of concern as Chris went into his "stricken stretcher-case" act.

"Oh dear! What's wrong with him?" . . . "The lad's ill!" . . . "Call a policeman!" . . . "Are you all right?"

Chris was rolling his eyes and clutching his chest dramatically. "It's m-m-my cardiac. . . . I—I sometimes have these attacks!"

A bobby and a policewoman came rushing over. "I'll keep an eye on him!" the bobby told his companion. "Ring up the station and have them send an ambulance straightaway!"

The Changing of the Guard was still going on in all its pomp. Drums beating, feet clumping, hoarse voices bellowing commands—then the slow march as the old guard and new guard approached each other for the handing-over of the keys. Mentally Chris apologized to the whole brigade for upstaging their show.

The ambulance arrived, its siren dying to a plaintive whine as it screeched to a halt at the curb. Chris was examined by a puzzled, white-coated intern, then lifted onto a stretcher.

"Easy, lad!" said one of the attendants.

Just as they loaded him into the ambulance,

Chris noticed the Royal Standard fluttering above the palace. It meant the queen was at home. "Wonder if she caught my act," Chris thought.

Then the doors were slammed shut and the ambulance roared off. In the distance, Chris could hear the faint strains of the band striking up "The British Grenadier."

"Well, it's a nice send-off, anyhow," he mused.

Events at the hospital proved a trifle more embarrassing. It took a full three-quarters of an hour of red tape, an electrocardiogram, and a discreet phone call to the Department of Danger before Chris could get himself released.

It was past one o'clock when he joined Spice and Geronimo at the restaurant where they had agreed to meet.

"What did that guy fire at you with his trick camera?" Geronimo asked.

"Some kind of metal needle. Poisoned, I assume. Folliott's sending a couple of men to look for it."

"Gerry spotted the fellow right after it happened," Spice reported. "But he got away before Sitting Bull could scalp him."

"Just as well," said Chris. "That way, TOAD has no tipoff that I was being covered."

"You reacted pretty fast. They might get suspicious."

Chris grinned dryly. "After all, a TOAD courier's supposed to keep his eyes open, isn't he? Can I help it if I'm quick-witted?"

"Look, Chris! Let's be serious." Spice's green eyes deepened with concern. "You know for sure now that TOAD has you measured for a coffin. Do you still intend to try to make contact and get hold of that package for Nikos?"

Chris shrugged. "That's the main reason Q sent me over here, isn't it?"

"He didn't order you to get yourself killed uselessly!"

"Well, somehow I'll have to convince them that I'm their man. The job's important and it has to be done. Besides, I'm committed now to see this thing through for the Department of Danger."

Spice looked at him for a long moment, then gave up with a sigh. "Okay, cool cat. So you'll be keeping your date with Little Miss Pamela at the Wax Museum this afternoon, right?"

"Right. I'll play lost and perhaps she'll put in a good word for me at TOAD." Chris finished his apricot trifle and took a sip of coffee. "But first I've a chat scheduled with Agatha, Duchess of Soho, at three o'clock."

Geronimo grinned. "Quite a busy social calendar in London."

"One gay, mad round," Spice added.

At Hyde Park the afternoon assortment of

soapbox orators, hecklers, and onlookers were slowly gathering in Speakers' Corner, across from the Marble Arch. Chris took in the faces and accents of the crowd—East Indian, West Indian, cockney, African, American.

His eyes stopped suddenly on a stout, tweed-skirted figure. "Ah, there you are, pussycat!"

He walked up behind her and cleared his throat. "Do forgive my barging up like this, but you *are* the Duchess of Soho, I pre—"

The twinkle died from Chris's eyes as the lady turned. She wasn't Agatha, Duchess of Soho!

Or *was* she? The shapeless hat, the bird's nest of brindle hair, the clothes—they all jibed. But instead of a lorgnette, she was peering at him through thick-lensed bifocals, and her upper lip failed to cover a mouthful of buckteeth.

"I beg your pardon, young man?"

"Um—er—I'm sorry, ma'am. Guess I made a mistake. I thought you were someone else."

The glasses gave the woman a disturbing impression of high-powered twin headlights. Chris backed away, mumbling apologies.

"Am I nuts? Or is she?" The TEEN agent thought. The woman had to be Agatha. The coincidence was too much. But if so, why the bifocals and the buckteeth? An easy disguise, of course, but why?

Chris was sure his own disguise was no barrier to recognition under the circumstances, especially since she had even recognized his voice over the phone. But she might have another, very good reason for taking cover! "Enemy agents, maybe!" Chris realized.

He edged cautiously away from the crowd to a more sheltered spot among some trees. From there, he gazed around watchfully.

His practiced eye could detect no one who looked like a possible TOAD agent. He glanced at his watch—3:12. Nobody else resembling Agatha was anywhere in view. Chris's sixth sense warned him to leave.

He circled through the park, then went out by the Grosvenor Gate. Finally, after doubling back and forth to make sure he wasn't being shadowed, he joined the other two TEEN agents at a "Wimpy Bar." Geronimo was munching a London hamburger and Spice was enjoying an early tea.

Chris reported his experience in Hyde Park.

"We're getting nowhere fast," Geronimo said gloomily.

"Courage, friends. Let us not throw in the towel till I've talked to Pamela."

Chris ordered tea, and the trio spent the next half hour or so laying their plans carefully. At last they left the Wimpy Bar and caught a taxi.

The afternoon was turning dark. The sky had clouded over, and a fog was sweeping in over London from the Thames. Chris got out of the cab two blocks from Madame Macabre's and walked the rest of the way. He wanted to arrive alone. Geronimo and Spice would keep the place under surveillance.

He bought a ticket at the museum and went inside. A jovial guard smiled at him at the entrance to the Gallery of Living History which occupied all the main floor. Chris was about to smile back and drop a friendly remark when he realized the guard was a wax dummy.

"Yerks!" thought Chris. "These jokers are a little *too* lifelike."

Inside was an eye-popping array of figures. Famous kings and queens of England—Richard the Lion-Hearted, Henry VIII, Good Queen Bess, Victoria. Then more recent heads of state. Churchill in his coveralls with a big cigar. President Franklin D. Roosevelt with his opera cape and jaunty cigarette holder. Stalin. Hitler. John F. Kennedy. Sport champions followed. Russian and American astronauts. . . .

"Chris!"

The TEEN agent turned and saw Pamela. "Ciao, baby," he said with a grin. "How quietly you sneak up on one!"

"A good thing, too. I'd just as soon not advertise this little rendezvous." She had left off her insect glasses and was looking very girlish.

Pamela glanced around nervously. "Let's go downstairs where it's nice and dim."

Downstairs was the House of Horrors. Marat being stabbed in the bath. Marie Antoinette on the guillotine. Jack the Ripper in action.

"You realize I'm risking my neck to help you?" Pamela murmured.

"Don't think I don't appreciate it," said Chris. "But I would like a wee inkling of what you have in mind."

Pamela's eyes flitted uneasily about the long dimly lighted chamber. "I think I can get you out of the country safely."

"Look, Pamela," Chris pleaded. "If I get back to the States mission unaccomplished, I'm finished with TOAD over there. Can't you get your people here to listen to me without pulling a gun right away?"

"I'll try. But your place isn't safe. You'd better hide out somewhere else."

"Like where?"

"Just trust me, will you?"

"Who could look in those big, baby-blue eyes and say No?" Chris replied. "Not to mention the fact that I haven't much other choice."

Pamela said the next step was to wait. They wandered about the chamber with the other museum visitors, looking at the wax dummies of famous murderers.

Presently the visitors began to thin out as closing time neared. Seizing her chance when no one was looking, Pamela steered Chris aside into a small storage closet and closed the door.

"What's the idea?" he whispered.

"Sh-h-h! You'll see."

Soon they could hear the voices of the museum attendants shepherding out the last visitors and locking up for the night.

Pamela and Chris sat side by side in the darkness. An hour passed. Finally Chris detected a faint, spooky noise in the outer chamber.

"Time to go," Pamela said.

They got up and emerged cautiously from the closet. Chris switched on his pocket flashlight and played it over the eerie wax figures.

In spite of himself, he shuddered at the sight of Simon Taw, the Liverpool murderer. Had the dummy moved? There was something oddly familiar about that thick-set figure and whiskery face. . . .

Chris stifled a sudden yelp. The dummy had just smiled at him! Then its hand moved and pulled off the beard.

"Colonel Buttram!"

"Good evening, my dear chap," said the colonel, fingering his mustache. "Sorry I had to keep you waiting so long."

Something hard pressed into the small of Chris's back and he heard Pamela giggle.

"April fool, Chris baby! Isn't it cozy, the way we've trapped you? TOAD always does these things with so much style!"

17 · Sniper's Hand

So HE HAD walked straight into a TOAD trap! Well, at least Geronimo and Spice would follow wherever Buttram would take him.

Chris sighed. "Really, Pamela! What a tatty trick to play on your trusting boy friend."

"My dear fellow," said Colonel Buttram, "you should feel honored! As Chief of British TOAD, I don't usually take part in tuppenny operations of this sort. But your case interested me so much, I decided to oversee it personally."

"The pleasure is all yours, I'm afraid, Colonel," said Chris.

Buttram produced a handsome, pearl-handled firearm and a flashlight of his own and kept Chris covered while Pamela taped his wrists.

Then she gagged him with a twisted silk handkerchief.

With a chuckle, Colonel Buttram walked over
to a corner of the room and lugged back the
original statue of Simon Taw.

"You must forgive my little prank," he said to
Chris. "Having picked a wax museum as the
scene of our trap, I couldn't resist giving you a
bit of a start just now. Spot of humor, you know."

The colonel guffawed heartily. "I trust Madame Macabre won't object to our use of her
premises in this fashion. Simply stole a few keys
from one of the guards on his way home."

He prodded Chris with his pearl-handled con-
vincer. "Now then, lad—out you go!"

They went up a stairway to the back door and
out into a high-walled yard. The sky was pitch
dark with only a pale, ghostly glow of light from
the street and buildings around them.

Through the thick, swirling fog, Buttram's
flashlight beam revealed a black van standing in
the yard. Chris was ordered to climb in. The
doors were locked and the van rolled away into
the night.

"Think positive now, boy!" he reminded himself. Keeping track of the turns, Chris got the impression they were heading in a northerly direction. Some time later the van seemed to go down
into a tunnel. He could hear the rumble of the
wheels echoing back from the walls.

Then they came to a stop. Sounds of a heavy metal door sliding open. The van moved forward again briefly, then stopped and the doors of the cargo compartment were opened. "End of the line, lad." Colonel Buttram gestured. "Out!"

Another man, pug-nosed with a cauliflower ear, whom Chris took to be the driver, stood by watching. Pamela was nowhere in sight.

Chris looked around curiously. They were in a concrete-walled garage containing several other vehicles—one of them a black Bentley.

"Move," said Buttram, prodding Chris again. "Straight ahead."

Entering a small, modern elevator, they rose to a higher level and stepped out into a room furnished like a doctor's surgery. Its two windows were curtained but open to the night air and slight wisps of fog came drifting in.

Beyond the room was an office. A dark, slender, bearded man, with close-set, sinister-looking eyes, stood near the doorway.

"Ah, Vignelli!" Buttram greeted him. "So you arrived from Geneva, eh? And how go things at our Central Directorate?"

"Well enough," the dark man said curtly. He nodded his head at Chris. "And who is this?"

"Our courier from North American Wing. Or perhaps I should say *pseudo*-courier."

Buttram pressed a button and two men came hurrying into the surgery. Both wore black turtle-neck sweaters under white lab smocks. One removed Chris's gag and untaped his wrists. Then Chris was ordered to strip to his shorts.

Before obeying, Chris paused to chafe his wrists and managed to flick the stem of his watch from Emergency Transmit to Off. It was fortunate that he did so, because the watch was taken away as soon as he undressed. The two attendants slung him roughly onto a white-sheeted table and pinioned his arms and ankles.

Colonel Buttram stood at an electronic console and flicked a switch. Chris jerked under the jolt of electricity. He was terrified.

"Bit of a tickle, eh?" Buttram said. "Actually that's just a mild foretaste of what's to come if you don't answer my questions."

"I'll do my best," Chris replied. To himself he repeated, "Keep cool. Control yourself!"

The first question came quickly. "What happened at Kennedy Airport before you took off for London?"

"I got picked up by FBI agents. They took me downtown and asked me a flock of questions."

"What about?" Buttram inquired.

"My family background. What I'm studying at school. My father. Stuff like that."

"And you were able to answer them?"

"Sure. Why not? I'm Chris Cool—I know all about myself, don't I? Anyhow, they let me go and BOAC booked me on a later flight."

"Why didn't you report all this to Nikos?"

"How could I?" Chris retorted. "I had no way to reach him—not even a phone number."

Buttram scowled thoughtfully. "All right. Now—about Lustig. What happened there?"

Chris told him.

"You got no look at whoever had been there before you?"

"No."

"Very well," said Buttram. "Which brings us to Dracov. Has he tried to contact you?"

"Let's say I contacted him . . . or tried to." Chris calmed his rapid breathing somewhat and continued. "They put a tail on me. That guy Peveny. I worked him over a bit, and he promised to fix up a meeting with Dracov. It was to be at the British Museum, but the cops got there first."

"And that business at the gunsmith's yesterday—how did that come about, eh?"

"Peveny had flown the coop by the time I broke out of the hospital. His landlady gave me Musgrave's address. It was written on a scrap of paper he left in his room." Chris paused and added, "All right if *I* ask a question?"

"Ask away," said Buttram.

"A guy in a car must've followed me when I left Musgrave's. Tailed me all the way to the rooming house where I was holed up. A gray Humber. Was it TOAD's?"

Buttram shook his head. "Not ours. Must've been Peveny's—or someone covering him. In point of fact, I was to meet him at Musgrave's for a bit of a powwow. We'd set the meeting up with Dracov. The Humber probably went along to give Peveny backup support."

"I see. Well, anyhow," Chris went on, "another Dracov man jumped me at Shepherd Market last night. Some joker with an RAF mustache. We had a friendly tussle and I took his dart gun away. Then we started out in a car to meet Dracov, but two guys in a black Bentley rammed us. Your boys, I suppose—only I wasn't sure at the time. Besides, I figured it was safer to act scared, in case word got back to Dracov. They might get wise that I was working for TOAD. So I took off."

Meanwhile, the two lab attendants had emptied the pockets of his clothes. One handed the sleepy-sliver pen to Buttram. "Apparently it fires anesthetic darts, sir."

Buttram and Vignelli both examined it. "Where'd you get this little toy?" the colonel asked Chris.

"The Dracov man last night. I told you I took his dart gun away."

"And this wrist-watch radio?" Buttram pursued as the other attendant handed it to him.

"Same place. The guy slipped it to me right after we were rammed. Told me to call Dracov over it, and I'd be given further orders about where to meet. I tried three or four times but no one responded. I suppose he forgot to give me the password call signal, or something."

Buttram opened the watch case and called for a magnifying glass. After examining the micro-circuitry inside, he dialed the stem into Voice Transmit position. "Try calling again," he whispered, holding the watch near Chris's lips.

"Christopher Cool calling Dracov. . . . Christopher Cool calling Dracov. . . . Come in, please!" The open use of his name was an urgent TEEN code signal that something was wrong, and that the caller was in enemy hands.

As he had expected, there was no response.

Buttram switched off the watch and handed it back to the attendant.

"Why waste time?" Vignelli broke in impatiently. "His information is not particularly useful. Dispose of him."

Chris turned his head to flick away the beads of sweat trickling over his face. His eyes suddenly widened. A hand holding a Luger pistol was reaching into one of the windows!

"Look out!" he yelled instinctively.

The TOAD men flung themselves to the floor as a shot thundered through the room. With split-second reflexes the two lab attendants and the van driver began firing back. Then, as the assassin's hand was withdrawn, they leaped to their feet and dashed out of the room in pursuit.

Buttram and Vignelli rose from the floor. The colonel's ruddy face had gone pale, and he brushed one hand across his cheek. "Ruddy near creased me, that shot did! You yelled just in time, laddie buck."

A few minutes later the three TOAD henchmen returned. "Dracov agent," one reported. "He'd jiggered the alarm system. We've taken care of him. B-12 says it's the same bloke that was sighted casing the layout last week."

Buttram chuckled coldly. "The Dracov Network's getting a bit above itself these days, I'd say. We shall have to do something about that."

"Meanwhile, what about this one?" Vignelli nodded his head toward Chris. "We've wasted enough time, in my opinion. Kill him!"

"Come, come old boy. Can't do that. Lad just saved my life!"

Vignelli's face showed cold disapproval. "Am I to understand that you wish me to report to the Central Directorate that you are parolling a possibly dangerous double agent?"

"No. But right now"—Buttram grinned slyly—"young Cool might still be very useful to us."

"How?"

"I have an idea. Let me think some more about it."

Chris was unstrapped from the table, photographed, and fingerprinted. Then Buttram told him to put on his clothes. As Chris tucked his shirt into his trousers, he managed to rip off the bottom shirt button and let it drop down his pant leg to the floor. With a nudge of his foot, he kicked it out of sight in the general direction of the adjoining office.

"Lock him up for the night," Buttram ordered. The attendants took Chris down a hallway to a windowless room. A recessed ceiling light filled the cell with a pale glow. The furnishings consisted of a table, chair, and cot.

"Someone's probably watching me on a TV monitor," Chris thought.

Kicking off his shoes and loosening his tie, he stretched out on the cot, hands clasped behind his head. One finger pressed the button at the back of his Ivy League shirt collar. This was a tiny radio receiver, capable of picking up the transmission from the button bug which he had dropped.

The pressure of Chris's finger switched on the receiver, which had a length of wire antenna woven into the shirt fabric.

A faint voice reached Chris's ear—the voice of Vignelli, no doubt speaking from the office adjoining the surgery. "I think, Colonel Buttram, it is now time for a full report on your project with Wong Hsiu. The Central Directorate is most interested in this matter."

"Quite so," Buttram's voice replied. "As you

know, Wong was a top Red Chinese biochemist.
But he was dissatisfied and wanted greater re-
wards, especially when he began getting close to
success on the Z-factor formula."

"Which is?"

"The Z-factor, as we call it—its Chinese name
being quite unpronounceable—is a chemical
agent for bringing about mutations in living
organisms. Mutations which result in giant
growth. Applied to pests such as insects, which
breed rapidly, this could result in a terrifying
threat to human life. Can you imagine, for ex-
ample, an enemy country overrun by giant ants?
I decided that such a weapon would make a
very useful addition to our TOAD arsenal. So I
took steps to obtain it."

"Most enterprising of you," said Vignelli.

"Through our Hong Kong contacts," Buttram
went on, "we had Wong smuggled out of China
and brought to England. In return for a laboratory setup here, and a price of one million
pounds sterling, Wong agreed to turn over his
formula to us as soon as it was perfected."

"And did he perfect it?"

"He did. Then came a bad setback. One of his
lab specimens got loose and nearly killed him.
Wong was found by the police, badly mauled,
and is now in the hands of the British author-
ities. Since then, we've been unable to decipher
his lab notes and all we have on hand is a small

amount of the Z-factor chemical. My technical men haven't been able to analyze it so far."

"I see," Vignelli said coldly. "And what is American TOAD's part in this project?"

"Nikos made a deal with me to underwrite half the cost of the project. I sent three giant hornets to him on one of our smuggling vessels as proof that the formula worked. They were to be turned loose offshore and home on an ultrasonic signal. Unfortunately"—Buttram gave a rasping cough—"Nikos's men who were to receive the insects were nabbed by the American police. We've no idea what happened to the hornets."

"A badly run operation," said Vignelli. "The Directorate will be most displeased."

"Luck of the game, you know. The Dracov Network also had its eyes on Wong and guessed who brought him here to England. That was why Dracov called on Lustig Tuesday—to discuss a deal."

"A deal, you say?" Vignelli asked sharply.

"We've no idea what their proposition was. Lustig thought he could handle things with just the defense weaponry at his flat. He was wrong. Dracov double-crossed him somehow and left Lustig half-dead on the floor."

"Another piece of bungling!"

"The game's not over yet," Buttram grated.

"Now then, let us go on to this affair of Dr. Jonathan Cool," said Vignelli. "Some time ago, through our Intelligence grapevine, the Central Directorate learned that something was brewing with regard to Dr. Cool. Something which smelled most important—perhaps profitable. His Red captors had hired the Dracov Network to contact Dr. Cool's son."

Chris's whole body tensed at the revelation. So his father *had* been kidnapped! And he must still be alive!

"As you know," Vignelli went on, "Dr. Cool is one of the world's top atomic scientists—potentially a most valuable piece of merchandise. Therefore, TOAD felt it worth while to find out exactly what was in the wind."

"So you arranged to slip in a double, eh?"

"Exactly. We ordered Nikos to check up on Cool's son and prepare one of his dead-men couriers by plastic surgery to resemble the youth."

"And what about the real Christopher Cool?"

"It appeared that Dracov would probably attempt to reach him through the Atomic Research Institute where his father had worked. So by drugs and brainwashing, Nikos subverted the secretary of the Institute's personnel manager and ordered her to alert him at the first sign of a communication to Dr. Cool's son."

Another voice cut in—evidently some TOAD underling. "Call from Geneva, sir!"

"I'll take it here," said Vignelli. "And shut that door when you go out, please."

Chris groaned inwardly. So much for his eavesdropping. The button bug was highly sensitive—one of Pomeroy's slickest pieces of work —but not sensitive enough to pick up a conversation through a closed door.

An hour passed. Chris finally fell asleep. He was awakened the next morning by a guard bringing breakfast on a tray.

Chris had barely finished eating when the door was unlocked for a second time. Colonel Buttram and Pamela stepped into the room.

"Morning, Chris," the blonde greeted him. "How'd you like to stretch your legs and do a bit of London sightseeing? I've a nice little expedition planned for us!"

18 · Tricks at the Tower

"A SIGHTSEEING TOUR? Sounds charming," said Chris. "But then almost anything would, compared to sitting in this safe-deposit vault."

"Like a bit of a wash-up first, I expect," Buttram remarked, and beckoned to an armed guard who was standing in the hall. "Oh, by the way," he added to Chris, "don't bother putting on your shirt."

Chris was escorted down the hall to a bathroom, the guard keeping him covered from behind. When they returned to the cell, Buttram pulled from his vest pocket a roll of tape and a small metal device about the size of a pillbox and taped it on Chris's chest.

"What's this for?" Chris asked.

"It's a bomb, actually. Clever little rig. Small but quite powerful enough to kill you. It's designed to be detonated by a radio signal. Pamela will be carrying a tiny transmitter which can trigger the thing at a moment's notice."

"Ah, I see. If I try cutting up rough—*boom!*"

"Exactly. Thing's made to implode like a bazooka charge and concentrate the blast. Blow a hole right through you, I'm afraid, but not apt to harm anyone else."

"Well, that's thoughtful," said Chris. "Just how many times *has* TOAD tried to kill me?"

"Hm! Let me see." Buttram counted on his fingers. "Four, if I recall rightly. That booby-trapped telephone in your hotel room. Then a rabid rat. And a needle-gun camera at the Changing of the Guard. Also, two of my men spotted you one night in a car and tried to get you."

The colonel frowned thoughtfully and ran fingertips across the bristles on his upper lip. "Almost five times, stop to think of it."

"Oh? How was that?"

"In Hyde Park yesterday. One of our agents spotted you and would have done the job then and there if you hadn't got the wind up."

So that explained Agatha's bucktoothed disguise, Chris reflected. The old girl must have spotted the TOAD agent and was trying to warn Chris off.

He put on his shirt, knotted his tie, and donned his blazer. "Well! Shall we away?"

The guard accompanied the young couple down to the garage. Pamela led the way to a dashing, open sports car—a sleek red Ghia, and took the wheel. Chris slid in on the other side. The guard pressed a button, opening a door in one wall, and they rolled out into a tunnel.

"Aren't you afraid I may do something desperate?" Chris asked.

"Don't try it," said Pamela. "I can trigger that bomb without even taking my hands off the wheel."

The tunnel continued for about two hundred yards. Then the car rolled up a ramp and into another garage. From here they emerged into the street.

Looking around, Chris guessed they were in Hampstead, a London suburb. Gloomily he reminded himself that his wrist-watch bleep signal over the Emergency Transit Channel the night before would have been cut off as soon as the van entered the tunnel.

The arrangement had been that if he and Pamela left the Wax Museum together, Geronimo and Spice would follow the signal in their taxi, using a small loop-antenna direction finder affixed to one of their wrist watches.

But the darkness and the fog would have made

their task doubly difficult. And once the signal cut out, any likelihood of them finding Buttram's headquarters was small indeed.

"Still, there's always the odd chance," Chris told himself with dogged hope. "My watch did bleep from the surgery for a little while." And, of course, there was always the shirt-button radio.

The car sped across London. Presently London Bridge loomed on their right over the Thames River . . . then the Tower Bridge and, flanking it on the waterfront, the grim, dirty, gray-white Tower of London.

Pamela parked and they walked across the square to buy admission tickets.

"Forgive me if I seem nosy," said Chris, "but just why have we come here?"

"But, dahling, this is a famous old heap of history! A must for every tourist!" said Pamela. "Surely you've heard? The spot where they did all the beheadings—Anne Boleyn, the Earl of Essex, and that lot?"

Chris nodded and wondered. Was TOAD using him as a decoy for some purpose?

They crossed the moat and passed over the Traitors' Gate. Then they went up into the Wakefield Tower for a look at the Crown Jewels. The glittering royal ornaments were displayed in a tall, eight-sided glass case in the center of the chamber—jewel-studded crowns, scepters, and swords; the Queen's Orb; even tankards and salt cellars were encrusted with gems.

Chris saw Pamela furtively attach a tiny gadget to the wall as they walked slowly around the display case with the other spectators.

"What's that?" he whispered. "Another bomb?"

"Ask me no questions, and you won't go boom!"

Afterward, the two walked up through the Bloody Tower, where Anne Boleyn's ghost supposedly roams at night, carrying her head under her arm. Then they sauntered around the grassy enclosure.

"I think we've soaked up enough history for one morning, don't you?" said Pamela.

Chris shrugged. They went back out across the moat to their car. A folded sheet of paper was tucked under the windshield wiper. Pamela plucked it out, unfolded it, and after a glance handed the message to Chris. It said:

Look at the black limousine across the street. You are both covered. Walk toward it and keep your hands in plain sight.

Chris looked. The limousine was over there, all right. Its rear windows were curtained, but the uniformed chauffeur smiled and touched his cap. His left hand was resting on the wheel.

Something peeped out from his glove hand and it seemed to be aimed in their direction.

"Is that a gun he's holding?" murmured Pamela.

"It's not a peashooter," said Chris. "I think we'd better walk over."

The back door of the limousine swung open and a bushy mustache and a toothy grin peered out. "Do come in, won't you?" invited Ringay. He, too, was armed.

Pamela got in, then Chris. A glass panel slid open in the partition separating the back seat from the driver's seat.

"Now hold out your hands, please," said Ringay. "You first, dear. Then the young man."

The chauffeur reached back and handcuffed Pamela and Chris while Ringay kept them covered. Then Ringay slipped black elastic blindfolds over their heads.

"May I ask how you knew we'd be here?" Pamela inquired.

"Trailed you all the way from Hampstead. I'm surprised a smart girl like you didn't notice—but I suppose you were chatting gaily with our young Mr. Cool."

The limousine started off. Chris sensed they were heading southward, over the Tower Bridge.

After a long ride, the car stopped. Getting out, Chris caught a whiff of lilacs and greenery, and the faint twittering of birds. They were some-where in the suburbs, no doubt.

The two young prisoners were herded into a building and seated side by side on what felt like a sofa. Then their blindfolds were removed, and Ringay left.

Chris's eyes widened. They were in a pleas-antly furnished drawing room. But what more immediately fixed his attention was a stout, horsy figure looming before them.

Agatha, Duchess of Soho!

"Don't tell me you're working for Dracov?" he gasped in amazement.

"I *am* Dracov, young man," she said in her deep, hoarse voice. "Lady Dracov, some call me."

No gold lorgnette or bifocals this time. Just her own two beady eyes, cold and hard as dia-mond drills. No buckteeth, either.

Chris took a deep breath and settled back on the sofa. "Well, in that case," he said, "here I am. Handcuffs and all. Now that we've finally got together, what's this 'information of great importance' you have for me? Something about my father, I hope."

Madame Dracov was carrying an English lady's walking stick. She slapped it casually across her open palm. "We'll have some infor-mation from you first. You can start by explain-ing how you came to be so chummy with TOAD."

"TOAD?" Chris echoed. "You mean that—that international spy ring—or crime syndicate?"

"That's what I mean. Lustig, for instance—one of their top dons. What were you doing at his place in Hatton Garden Tuesday night?"

"Before I left the States, I got a message from someone named Nikos advising me to visit Lustig in London. It was all very mysterious. I thought maybe he could tell me something about Dad, too. Only he was in no shape to talk when I got there, so I had to scram. But I guess you know all about that if you read the papers."

"Oh, I read the papers. Especially the Personal Columns. That's how I saw your ad mentioning the 'rare insects.' "

Chris nodded. "The message from Nikos said to use that as a password. It sounded as if more than one person was involved, so after I started dodging the law, I inserted that Personal notice, hoping Lustig's friends might help me."

Lady Dracov's eyes remained cold. "Quite a yarn. I might have swallowed it, if I didn't find you keeping company with this TOAD dolly."

Chris's jaw dropped open in faked astonishment. "TOAD dolly? Are you kidding? Her uncle's a friend of your boy Peveny's. Then I ran into Pamela at a discotheque, and we—well, we sort of fell for each other. She fixed me up with a place to hide out. At her uncle's house."

"Colonel Buttram, sonny boy, is the Chief of

British TOAD. Still, you might be simple enough to be taken in—though I frankly doubt it from the way you and your chum handled Peveny."

"How do *you* know so much about TOAD?" Chris asked innocently.

"It happens we're in the same business. One has to know one's competition."

"By 'same business' you mean espionage, I suppose," Chris said. "Well, if you've learned anything about my father, let's hear it. And incidentally, why didn't you contact me right away at the Thackeray Arms Hotel?"

"Because we found out a TOAD man had been snooping about the room we reserved for you there. So we decided to lie low and keep a watch on you till we found out what was what."

"I see. So our meeting at the restaurant wasn't just an accident. You were sizing me up?"

Lady Dracov nodded. "You were trailed from the time you left the hotel. I slipped into the restaurant behind you, just long enough to order a cup of tea and drop that fly in your soup as the waiter passed my table."

Chris looked puzzled. "What *is* all this jazz about insects? An act you put on for cover?"

"Not quite. If you're all that ignorant, maybe your little girl friend can enlighten you." She prodded Pamela with her stick and added, "TOAD's onto something, you see. Something big—a formula for a new weapon of biological warfare, eh sweetie? And it has to do with insects, judging from one or two clues I've picked up."

"Ah! I'm beginning to get the picture!" Chris snapped his fingers. "Peveny's landlady gave me an address he'd left in his room. A gunsmith's shop. That's where I first met Pamela's uncle. If he's Chief of British TOAD, as you say, maybe you were sending Peveny to meet him there—to talk about this formula. Right?"

Lady Dracov fixed him with her gimlet eyes again. "You're getting smarter."

"And the gray Humber that trailed me to the rooming house—was that one of your men?"

"Right again. I phoned the number in the ad to find out if it was you. Then, after the Humber man called to report about gassing your chum, I had Peveny phone you to fix up a contact."

"You never intended to keep our date at Hyde Park?" Chris asked.

"Certainly. Only a TOAD man was watching me at the park, so I had to shoo you off."

"But how cleverly you turned the tables," Pamela put in admiringly. "You had *our* man trailed back to the house in Hampstead, and then sent a killer to rub out Colonel Buttram. Except that he ran into a spot of trouble, I'm afraid."

Lady Dracov snorted, "No great loss. We staked out the neighborhood this morning, and you two walked right into our arms!"

"Hold it, please," Chris interrupted. "I'm still waiting to hear about my father."

"Your old man is a prisoner behind the Iron Curtain. The country that's holding him hired my network to deliver you, for a nice fat hundred thousand dollars."

"You mean that letter you sent to the Institute was just bait to get me over here?"

"What else? Much safer and simpler to put the snatch on you here than in America. Saves us half the freight charges—let alone cutting down the risk—if you come halfway under your own power."

"But why? What's the angle?" Chris inquired. "I'm no atomic physicist!"

"Neither is your father, for all the good he's doing them. From what I hear, he has nerves like granite. They can't squeeze any atomic secrets out of him, and he absolutely refuses to do any research for them. My hunch is they want you as a hostage—to break his will and force him to do what they ask."

Chris's mind whirled. "If you could have cashed in on me, why did you wait so long?"

"To get the package for Nikos in the bargain, if possible. It's worth quite a bit more than a hundred G's."

Lady Dracov let out a harsh bray of laughter. "Now I have *both* you and Colonel Buttram's Girl Friday—who will soon tell us all she knows about TOAD's mysterious secret formula."

Lady Dracov flicked a tiny switch on her walking stick. A set of long, needle-like blades flashed out from the end of the stick and began to rotate at high speed. "Otherwise I may have to tattoo you the same way I tattooed Lustig!"

Pamela went white and shrank back as the blades moved closer and closer to her face.

She started to scream. Simultaneously there were the sounds of a commotion outside—muffled shots and the sounds of a struggle. Before Lady Dracov could reach the door, it burst open and she found herself facing Colonel Buttram and a squad of armed TOAD agents.

"Better drop that nasty little turkey carver, old girl," he warned, "unless you fancy a hole in the head!"

Buttram chuckled as his agents seized her. "By the way, thanks so much for taking our bait. I rather thought these two would entice you into showing your hand. It was no trick at all to follow them—Pamela's wired for sound!"

He ordered his men to round up the Dracov group. Then Pamela's handcuffs were removed and she and Chris were taken outside to a closed car. Buttram got in with them and it sped off.

"Events are moving fast, I'm afraid," he said.

"What's up?" Pamela inquired.

"Vignelli's been nabbed by British agents. They picked him up soon after he left the house. Apparently they're on the verge of closing in."

"Oh dear. How did that happen?"

"A tiny bug we discovered too late. Planted by our young friend here, I imagine." Buttram eyed Chris grimly. "The British Secret Service is ruthlessly efficient when they have to be. If they make Vignelli talk, it could be disastrous to TOAD. I think the time has come to put Plan Z into effect!"

19 · Terror Telecast

SPICE AND GERONIMO were ushered into Folliott's office. The girl's face looked pale after a nearly sleepless night. Geronimo's lank black hair was uncombed and his jaw was clenched.

"Please sit down," said Folliott. "Sorry I've had no time to keep you informed but I've been up all night directing search operations."

"What about Chris?" Spice asked anxiously.

"Still no word, I'm afraid. Let me go back and review all that's happened. Friday night, after you gave us the general area from your radio direction-finder, my men moved into Hampstead and began a quiet, house-to-house check. Quite a sizable area to cover. The trans-

161

mission from Cool's button bug helped to narrow the search a bit, but its signal was intermittent —not enough to triangulate on."

"Pick up anything useful?" Geronimo inquired.

"No. Except we learned that Vignelli was there. Buttram had addressed him by name. Later one of my agents who had seen him in Switzerland spotted him in his car leaving Hampstead. Unfortunately the car was equipped with radio, and by the time we hunted him down TOAD had gotten warning."

Geronimo grunted. "They flew the coop?"

"Every man jack. By the time we finally did locate the house late yesterday, they were gone and all their papers burned. The exit, by the way, was through a long underground tunnel."

Spice looked at Geronimo. "So that's why Chris's signal cut out on Friday night!"

"Any leads yet on where they've gone?" Geronimo asked Folliott.

"None. Except that it may be somewhere in Kent near the scene of the monster attacks."

Folliott reached for a paper. "You know about TOAD's ultimatum to the Prime Minister?"

Geronimo nodded. "We heard a radio bulletin."

"The letter was mailed in London yesterday, stamped express and marked 'Highly Urgent.' It reached Downing Street last night. Letters were also sent to the newspapers. Here's a copy."

Spice and Geronimo both read it.

FROM: Chief of British TOAD
TO: The Prime Minister and People of England

1. The Nation faces a deadly peril.
2. A videotape is being sent to the British Broadcasting Corporation which shows the full nature of this peril and what can be done to avoid it.
3. It is suggested that this tape be telecast to the public at 12 noon tomorrow, Sunday.
4. Unless our terms are met within 24 hours after that time, H.M. Government will bear full responsibility for the horrible catastrophe which follows.

There was a knock on the door, and one of Folliott's aides entered, carrying some Sunday newspapers. "Seen any of these yet, Chief? They're all putting out special editions."

Folliott took them and glanced at the black banner headlines. "How about the editorials?"

"All the same line. They say the people faced Hitler's worst during the Blitz, and they have a right to know what we're up against this time. Therefore the tape must be broadcast."

Folliott nodded gloomily and started to speak when one of his telephones rang. "Folliott here. . . . Yes, sir. That's clearly understood. . . . Very good, sir."

He hung up and faced the others. "Well,

there's the answer. The Home Secretary has just given the BBC permission to run the tape."

Folliott looked at his watch. "Ten-twenty. We've a little more than an hour and a half to wait. What about a spot of tea, you two?"

A man brought in a steaming pot on a tray with cups, sugar, cream and lemon.

Spice asked, "How was the tape delivered?"

"By messenger to Broadcasting House in Portland Place," Folliott replied. "Lad on a motorbike. Said some man stopped him on the street and offered him a quid to deliver it."

"Have you seen it yet?" Geronimo put in.

"Yes, but I won't try to describe it. I would rather wait and let you two form your own reactions."

Shortly before noon, a television set was rolled into the office. At the stroke of twelve a sign was flashed on the screen, saying: ULTIMATUM TO THE PRIME MINISTER AND THE BRITISH PEOPLE. . . .

A BBC announcer's voice said, "As most of you know by now, an urgent message was received last night at Number 10 Downing Street . . ."

He went on to describe the events leading up to the telecast and ended, "For the time being, Her Majesty's Government will have no statement to make on this matter. The videotape follows."

A picture appeared of a door bearing the sign:

LABORATORY AREA

NO ADMITTANCE

EXCEPT AUTHORIZED TOAD PERSONNEL

The voice of Colonel Buttram offscreen began, "Beyond this door lies one of the most frightful new developments in biological warfare—a form of terror which we in TOAD earnestly hope need never be unleashed upon the English people. However, it is only fair that each and every one of you know the full extent of the danger."

The door opened and the TV camera dollied into the laboratory. "TOAD has in its possession a chemical which can cause living creatures of any sort to breed to enormous size. You will now see its effect on certain small pests which breed with great rapidity."

Spice gasped as the camera showed wire-mesh cages containing gigantic mosquitoes, wasps, hornets, houseflies, tsetse flies, and lice. A lab attendant, with hooded face, stood by to show the relative size of the monsters.

Buttram went on talking as the camera showed a huge, ferocious fire ant. "Even normal-sized fire ants will attack young birds and sting them to death. I leave you to imagine what a horde of these giant-sized ones might do to human beings."

But the worst was yet to come—enormous rats the size of full-grown hogs!

"One such rat," Buttram added, "has already broken loose and is ravaging livestock and endangering human life, as you have no doubt read."

He paused. "You have seen our weapons: frightful pests, breeding out of control, threatening all forms of life in our British island. Now, our proposition and our ultimatum.

"Yesterday British agents arrested a top TOAD executive, Pietro Vignelli. He must be released with a full apology. Furthermore, the British Crown Jewels must be handed over to TOAD in a manner to be described later.

"Unless this is done within twenty-four hours, our biological warfare chemical will be dropped into a public sewer. Soon huge rats will be breeding all over London . . . and the insect pests will multiply even faster.

"Once the chemical has been released, there can be no defense except utter extermination— an impossible task, as government scientists will affirm. In weeks or months all of Britain will be overrun by the horrors you have just seen!"

Chris stirred woozily on the bunk of his whitewashed cell. The drug which he had been given in his Sunday evening meal was now wearing off. His head ached and his limbs felt heavy.

A key grated in the lock, and the door of his cell swung open. An armed guard entered, followed by Colonel Buttram and Pamela.

"Well, laddie buck," said Buttram, "the twenty-four-hour deadline is almost up, and it appears Her Majesty's Government is about to yield."

"Don't make me laugh," Chris scoffed.

"Oh, but it's quite true," put in Pamela. "Remember that little thing you saw me stick on the wall at the Tower of London? It was a bug. Broadcasts everything that's said there. And we just now heard them removing the Crown Jewels—to be handed over to TOAD! Isn't that simply smashing?"

"I'm ecstatic," Chris said dryly.

"Only one flaw in the picture," Buttram added. "Your usefulness as a hostage is over now, old chap. However, take comfort—we at least have a most interesting fate planned for you!"

Chris was escorted down to a lower level of the TOAD base, then along a winding corridor. The group stopped before a metal door which Buttram unlocked. "Inside, laddie!"

As he obeyed, Chris felt Pamela press something into his hand. But he didn't pay much attention because his eyes were riveted on the two persons he saw standing inside the long concrete-walled room.

Spice! . . . Geronimo!

The door slammed, leaving them in darkness. But before either could reply, another door slid open at the far end of the room. In the faint light the TEEN agents saw three huge rats as big as mastiffs come scuttling in!

The creatures' eyes glittered in the gloom, and their long, curved teeth were like tusks.

Then the door from which the rats had emerged slid shut. Chris, Spice, and Geronimo were alone in the dark with the monsters!

20 · The Rat Race

THERE WAS NO time for talk. The repulsive beasts were already creeping toward their prey! Chris shuddered at the sounds of their blood-chilling squeaks and the scratchy noise of their claws on the concrete as the monstrous rats came closer.

How to fight off the brutes when every possible weapon had been taken away, and no doubt his companions' as well?

"Get behind us, Spice!" Chris reached out to pull her behind him and Geronimo.

Just then twin beams of intense, blinding light lanced out through the darkness, to be reflected back from the rats' eyes! Momentarily dazzled and frightened, the monsters scuttled off.

"How'd you do it, Spice?" Chris gasped.

"Gimmick earrings—Pomeroy's latest masterpiece. Same principle as that dazzler beam you used against the motor launch in the Moonfire caper. Luckily my lobes are pierced so the TOAD guards didn't bother taking my earrings before they shoved us in here!"

"Watch it!" Geronimo warned.

Two, three, four moments of panting suspense. The monstrous rats were squeaking again, their claws creeping closer as they gathered courage to renew the attack.

Again the twin beams of light flashed out and Geronimo cut loose with a bloodcurdling Apache war whoop. Once more the rats retreated, but the TEEN agents knew it was only a temporary respite.

"The power cells in my earrings are only good for four flashes," Spice murmured tensely, "and I have already used up two!"

Chris's palms were moist with perspiration. Suddenly he remembered the object which Pamela had pressed into his hand just before he was prodded into the room. He was still clenching it. The thing felt like a ring.

A ring!

"Oh, oh!" Chris's brain began clicking as coolly as ever. He'd been forgetting all sorts of things, a result of the drugs that had been injected to keep him quiet after being brought here to the TOAD base from Lady Dracov's lair and flung into a cell. And he'd forgotten the most important thing of all—the pillbox bomb that Buttram had tapped to his chest yesterday morning!

"The ring may be the radio transmitter gadget that Pamela carried for triggering the bomb!" Chris realized.

She had slipped it to him out of pity, no doubt. He could blow himself up quickly instead of letting those saber-toothed horrors do the job. The beasts once again were slowly crawling closer.

Another Apache yell from Geronimo split the darkness and Spice flashed her earring lights a third time.

As the rats scuttled off again, Chris was already tearing open his shirt. He ripped away the tape.

"Only one more flash left!" Spice warned in a shaky voice.

"Go ahead! Use it when you have to!" Chris said. "We'll need free space around the door!"

As he spoke, he taped the pillbox bomb to the door lock with desperate speed.

Spice's earrings fired their last brilliant flash, which fizzled quickly as the power cells gave out. But, coupled with Geronimo's war whoop,

the effect was startling enough to drive the rats
into one last, temporary retreat.

"Okay! Stand away from the door!" Chris
yelled. Hoping he had guessed right, he tried
to rotate the stone of Pamela's ring.

No action!

Chris pressed the stone inward. *Ka-boom!* The
bomb exploded and the door burst open, sagging
on its hinges!

"Come on!" Chris yelled. He pushed Spice
and Geronimo outside, then dashed after them.

The rats retreated, frightened afresh by the
sharp report of the blast. But they would sally
out soon!

Chris glanced back as the three TEEN agents
raced down the corridor. "Here they come!"

The first of the huge rats was already darting
out of the concrete room. The sight of its furry
bulk, clawlike feet, and twitching tail sent a
shudder through Chris. And the other two monsters were pressing close behind it!

Seeing their prey about to escape galvanized
the rats into action. They lunged in savage pursuit, covering ground at alarming speed.

The TEEN agents heard footsteps coming toward them from somewhere ahead, along the
winding corridor.

"TOAD guards!" Spice gasped. "They must
be coming to investigate the explosion!"

"This way!" Geronimo tugged her arm and

swerved aside into a branching corridor on their right. Chris stayed at their heels but turned his head to glimpse the main corridor behind them.

The TOAD guards, headed by Colonel Buttram, burst into sight. Then the group skidded to a halt. Their faces reflected terror as the huge rats leaped to attack. Guns fired wildly amid screams of the TOAD men.

By now the TEEN agents had reached a spiral iron stairway. Spice darted up it, followed by Geronimo and Chris. Shots and moans were still echoing through the corridors below.

Just across from the top of the stairwell was an office. A uniformed guard rose from his desk, eyes popping in surprise as the three young Americans came rushing in.

Spice grabbed the plaster figure of a toad off the top of a file cabinet and hurled it at him. The guard ducked and tried to yank out his gun. Before the weapon could clear its holster, Geronimo had leaped over the desk and leveled him with one blow.

Chris locked the door. No one in sight yet! Spice, meanwhile, had scooped a telephone off the desk and was dialing. "Calling Folliott!" she told Chris tersely.

She gave a rapid-fire report of the situation and the location of the TOAD base, then hung up.

Geronimo hoisted a window sash. "Outside!"

he ordered Spice. She climbed out fast and the boys followed as footsteps pounded in the corridor. Someone rattled the doorknob, then the butt of a carbine splintered the door.

But the TEEN agents were already scurrying through the shrubbery that bordered the brick mansion.

Panting, the trio paused.

"Better keep on the move," Geronimo advised. "They'll have the dogs after us soon."

"And the fence is electrified!" Spice added.

Chris nodded. "I know—I saw it when they brought me here." As they zigzagged among the trees and heavy underbrush, he added, "How did you two get caught?"

"We came out from London with a big force of police and soldiers," Geronimo explained. "Folliott's fanning them out all over Kent, trying to locate the TOAD setup. I was whipping around on a motorcycle with Spice in the sidecar when we spotted Pamela in her red Ghia."

"We chased her up a wooded lane," Spice went on, "and ran into the hands of TOAD."

Through the underbrush and foliage, they caught brief glimpses of armed guards rushing about the grounds. One guard ran toward the house with a brace of Great Danes on a leash.

"*Aiyee!* Things could get nasty!" Geronimo muttered.

A faint *chop-chop* noise drew their attention skyward. A transport helicopter was coming.

"Paratroops!" Spice squealed, then clapped a hand over her mouth in dismay as a guard turned at the sound.

He yelled and started to run in their direction. But he froze as the chopper drew overhead. Moments later, white parachutes blossomed in the air.

The battle that followed was short but lively. Shots were still being exchanged as armored cars converged on the TOAD estate.

When it was all over, Chris, Spice, and Geronimo sat in the TOAD office, listening to Folliott's account of the mop-up.

"Quite a haul," he told them with grim satisfaction. "Buttram and his top British TOAD staff and most of their key agents. Plus enough names and addresses to run down the others, including Nikos and his operation in the States. Also Lady Dracov and most of her network boys —they were imprisoned in cells down below."

"How about the rats and other assorted monsters?" Chris asked.

"They're all under control. And a squad of soldiers trapped and killed the rat that was loose, by the way. We also have the Z-factor chemical. Part of it will be sent to your chaps in Washington for analysis."

"Did you really intend to hand over the Crown Jewels?" Chris inquired.

Folliott shrugged. "Who knows? We found their bug in the Tower and let them think so, in hopes of buying more time."

"Time?" Spice echoed. "You almost got us fed to the rats because Buttram thought sure you were ready to knuckle under."

Folliott gave a sigh of relief. "Well, it didn't happen. However, these little hazards do arise . . . when one's working for the Department of Danger!"

GERONIMO
JOHNSON